To my Wife and my Son,

You light the darkest corridors.

Part I

I look down through the thick, convex floor-glass of our Commander's airship. Broken tousled husks of buildings that once reached into the clouds and melded their steel with puffs of weightless white litter the landscape. It was a strange harmony, but accordant nonetheless, at once displaying nature's quiet but powerful splendor and the culmination of humankind's marvelous and often misguided accomplishments. Now they lie on their sides, in two, in ten; some with holes large enough to fly this airship through, some with enough small holes to have looked like an army of giant metal-eating insects had bored a home into them. Battered, disemboweled, and forgotten. Every dead building breathed an arsenic grey fume that oozed from the fissures and chasms of the fractured frames. Hollow windows and broken floors, caved-in ceilings and splintered doors. Though no one would have ever marked the city as alive had it not been for the people within it, you could not mistake its carcass. Hundreds of cities lay lifeless just like this one; the inhabitants dead or gone someplace where they believed the imperious grasp of our inhumanity to ourselves could not reach them. It always seemed to. And every year there were fewer and fewer places unaffected by its suffocating grip. A grip that I knew I was only helping to tighten. The idealist in me thought that perhaps if it were tightened enough, the stifling hand would become too weak to maintain and break under the force of its own hold, letting the world breathe free again instead of this somber tired heaving. Morgan, my brother, felt the same. At least that's the impressions I had gotten from him the last time we spoke, when he left for the academy years before I realized I would follow in his footsteps. Before my reminiscing could get very far, Frankie "Fox" Machae, my friend through all four years of laborious but invigorating special ops training, puts his hand on my shoulder and smiles, his vibrant green eyes rife with anticipation.

"Time to throw down, right Jake?"

"Oh my god dude, Jason, *Jason*! I *hate* being called Jake, you *know* this how many times."

"Alright alright alright! Sheesh. Anyway…Jason…"

I crack a half sarcastic, half genuine smile and roll my eyes. He was a smug son-of-a-bitch, but a good friend, and an even better soldier. Only Todd Givvens and myself had scored higher at graduation evaluation.

"Aren't you excited man? This is our first deployment! Real action, guns blazing, bad guys droppin', the Lieutenant smiling at us with those luscious lips and those pearly whites."

"Dude stop it, that's disrespectful."

"Hey I'm just sayin' what is bro."

"That's how it starts but I know what the next step is and you ain't takin' it. Don't make me pull rank on you."

Machae becomes tense and abnormally serious. I sense the shift but can't hold my stone-faced stare more than three seconds before I start laughing.

"You're an asshole, JAKE…you know that."

"Only to you Fox, haha!"

"Hey you seen Jenkins around? Word has it he's got some inside info on the mission; don't know how he came by it."

Machae started to remind me of grade school days, when nothing was more attention grabbing than the latest rumor. It was strange to me that so close a correlation could be drawn between the boy he had been, and the 26 year old, highly trained, exceedingly effective soldier that stood before me. Perhaps that's how he balanced himself; how he figured best to deal with what he must have known would be hell on earth, before his eyes and through his weapon. Jenkins seemed to have a similar tendency though he was often too shy to show anything other than his timidity; another curious aspect for a soldier. Nevertheless, these men and I had strove for ten long years (six in a military academy, and four at the special ops training facility form where we had just departed for the first time since we were inducted) to become the best of the best. A meager 600 applicants were accepted into the program (which cycled only when the previous class from 4 years earlier was done) and only 200 would make it through to the end. There was even a fatality rate around .02%. It's higher than it sounds considering we'd never been within hundreds of miles of a battlefield. I trusted them with my life, and they trusted me with theirs. I was sure we were ready for any assignment, any mission command would dare throw at us. Ready, willing, and able.

"Dude, Jake…Jason, helloooo? Sergeant Magnusun, where'd you go?"

"Oh sorry Fox I…no I haven't seen Jenkins since we took off actually. Anyway the Lieutenant's gonna brief us in like three hours, what's the rush?"

"Hey I wanna feel smart when she starts breakin' it down for us you know like, I could point out the enemy's suspected coordinates and then she'd ask me how I did that and I could say, 'Well, that's just where I thought they'd be from a tactical standpoint. That's where I'd be!' "

"Something's wrong with you. Really, go…go get me a sandwich would you, I just realized I'm starving."

"Is that an order, sir?"

"No it's a command from your rightful lord and master, get a move on would ya?"

"Yeah yeah, I'm on it. Be back in a flash."

He strides off in his usual easy and confident gait and at the same moment one of my two corporals, alpha team (Jenkins and Machae) leader Gary Stevenson briskly approaches me, a look of urgency on his face.

"Stevenson what's up man what's…what's wrong you look…stiff."

His voice is deep and raspy, and could carry across a lecture hall with ease.

"We gotta do a serious equipment revamp. Apparently the Black Hand had some well-hidden anti-air emplacements near our original landing zone. Command has to drop us off about 20 clicks from the target."

"2 miles? That's messed up."

"It gets worse."

Stevenson moves in closer to me, his broad shoulders ending in thick arms that cast a shadow over my face as he holds up his tablet displaying a map of our zone of operations.

"We were expecting little to no resistance until we got inside the caverns right? Wrong. The Black Hand has a good portion of their 105th company stationed…around here; we're talking 130 enemies at least."

"Wow. Okay. So what do we have available to us?"

"Now that's the good news. You know the Mark Six prototype?"

"Uh, that's the…the new heavy cannon, the one with the extra long snout and the ridiculous rate of fire, right?"

"Yeah, we get to have one of those! I feel like a kid on Christmas."

"Okay but none of us have directly trained in its use."

"Well they told me it handles pretty much the same as the older models, it's just heavier and kicks a little more…and kills better. That's all they told me though so who knows but either way we're gonna need it."

"Agreed. What else?"

"They're giving us a double supply of D9 frags but we've gotta drop a couple of power packs to fit them."

"I don't know if that's such a good idea."

"Yeah, I was thinkin' that too…but the Mark Six should make up for it. We need extra grenades for crowd control."

"That makes sense I guess."

"So yeah, other than that our standard plasma rifles, pistols, knives, thermo-visors, rations, radios, flares, smoke grenades. I know those tin cans aren't usually part of your loadout but you might want to take one this time, just in case. I am."

"Duly noted."

"My team'll be handling the Mark Six, so no worries yeah? Update your team, I'm off to tell mine."

"Okay. Hey, Machae is getting me a sandwich, I'll tell him."

"Okay, thanks. See you at the briefing."

I knew I had to find my beta team leader, Todd Givvens, first. Officers are supposed to administrate. In other words no matter how menial or how intensive the task, I'm supposed to use the men and women under my command to take care of something first. Apparently it's more efficient but I always felt awkward telling someone else to do something I knew I could do myself. The more dangerous the task, the more reluctant I became. I was able to do it well enough in training because I knew the bullets weren't real. Now I wasn't sure I wanted to be giving any orders to anyone. I skipped down a small set of thin metal stairs, then turned left and passed through a steel-blue door outlined in black, then down another longer set of stairs to the operations center. As I had suspected, Todd was already at the large oval-shaped table, slouched in a flimsy mesh chair with a vacant stare. I call his name but get no response. I lean toward him and tap the table; he doesn't budge. I straighten myself, scrunch my brow, and tilt my head in bewilderment. Todd was always so focused and attentive; eager to learn, absorbing the knowledge heaped on him faster than our instructors could dump it. His vacuous gaze and the sheer ignorance of my presence was more than I was willing to deal with.

"Corporal Givvens!"

"Sir, yes sir!"

Immediately he snaps to attention and salutes.

"I was standing here for a full thirty seconds calling you, what's wrong solider?"

"Nothing sir I just…I was thinking about the mission sir."

"What about it?"

He pauses, rapidly blinking his eyes and grinding his teeth. His apprehension fills the room with a quiet tension; the kind that threatens to destructively erupt if not soon alleviated.

"You may speak freely Corporal."

"They haven't told us *why* we're doing this sir. We're the special operations division, we're the ones that're supposed to get this information, aren't we? Why would they send us in to check out a tunnel network, isn't this a job for the army commandos?"

"I'm not sure I follow you…"

"In these situations, the only reason they won't tell us what's in there is because we'd either break ranks and run if we knew, or because they don't think we're gonna make it. I don't like either one of those…sir."

"Todd, you know how the brass is, you think the regular army gets treated any differently? We're just the tip of the blade; the Commander and his officers are the hand holding it. The Lieutenant should tell us more at the briefing but get used to the lack of information, it's gonna be a staple in future missions. This isn't training camp anymore."

"Yes sir."

"Ironically, I came to tell you that the initial information concerning mission parameters was wrong."

"I fucking *knew* it…sir."

"We're expecting heavy resistance on the way to our main objective and in-ops discovered some AA near the primary landing zone, so they're dropping us at LZ Delta, 20 clicks from the target. We've got an equipment change too; I'll upload the list to your tablet now."

Remembering I had put it in my pocket instead of leaving it with my other equipment in my locker, I pulled out the 20 centimeter panel of plastic and glass, tapped the liquid crystal buttons on the bright multicolored screen and sent the information to the rest of the team's pads.

"Nothing too drastic, just some optimizing. The new info on enemy forces is there too. Go find Wheatly and Christiansen and let them know. Shouldn't be too hard to find them, where one is, the other's not far."

"Sir, yes sir."

Givvens turns on his heel in perfect military fashion and hurries off. I sit down in the closest chair to me, put my elbows on my knees, and drop my head into my waiting hands, simmering in my thoughts, waiting for Lieutenant Merridan to show.

"Oh hey, there you are. BLT, roast beef, your favorite."

Machae, who I didn't even hear come in, hands me the sandwich. It sits in my hand for a full two minutes before I take the first juicy, enlivening bite. Just as I swallow, Lieutenant Miranda Merridan, and our division's presiding officer, Commander Tritium, walk into the room. I toss the sandwich on the table and quickly stand, saluting them.

"As you were" Miranda says, still staring at the tablet in her hand.

I sit back down and my eyes locked on her shimmering sangria hair, swishing over her shoulders like Caribbean island waves. Machae wasn't lying about her lips either. I get so distracted that I barely notice the rest of the team filing into the room. Has it been that long already? Is it almost time? What exactly are we going down there for? Miranda answers all my questions.

"Okay, everyone's here, good. I know this is your first mission so try not to get yourselves killed before you've even got something to come back and brag about. We're moving up the timeframe to 1600 hours. There's a rainstorm over the area but command tells me it's isolated and should break up soon. As you know, the Black Hand militia has been growing exponentially as more and more cities run out of resources and fall into chaos. We have confirmed reports that a large contingent of troops and much of the core of the Hand's upper leadership is holed up in a subterranean base, something from the mid 2000's that was abandoned due to the shortages. Our primary objective is to infiltrate the base, plant explosives at key locations marked on the maps on your tablets, and collapse the whole thing on top of them. I'll have the charges with me and I'll wait to distribute them until after we reach the first placement marker in case we get separated beforehand. We're expecting moderate resistance near the entrance, and we *must maintain stealth* once we get inside the caverns that lead to the base. Secondary objectives include acquiring Intel, and rescuing any civilians they might be holding down there; reports on that are unconfirmed. Any questions?"

The team sits motionless, eyes fixed and enwrapped. I had expected to feel some amount of restiveness coming from my fellow soldiers, but what I felt instead was resignation. They knew, I knew, how difficult this mission would be, but still we were settled, and stalwart. Miranda suddenly shifts her gaze to me. Her incisive bright hazel eyes lock with mine and for a moment it seems that everyone else in the room disappears, leaving only the two of us trying to discern what the other is thinking. As quickly as the heartening feeling appeared, it evaporates.

"Okay then. Gear up; be at docking bay 2 in 40 minutes. If anything happens to me, Magnusun, you're in charge."

"Yes ma'am."

"Lieutenant or just L-T will be fine. Ma'am makes me sound girly, I don't consider myself girly, do I look girly, do I *feel* girly to you, Sergeant?"

"No ma, uhh, No Lieutenant. Not in the slightest."

"Good," she said, as she smiled sunnily, "wouldn't want you thinking that. See you on the dropship."

The curiousness of her words and the pragmatic way in which she spoke them left me fuddled. Not wanting to disrupt my readiness with unsuitable thoughts, I close my eyes and purge them, focusing until all I can envision is the view down the sight of my gun. I raise and drop my

~ 11 ~

shoulders with a gentle sigh and make my way to the equipment room with haste.

An hour later, the eight of us are strapped upright with tight black cloth belts to the walls of the cramped dropship. Wheatly and Christiansen are across from me on the far left, side-by-side, talking quietly to each other. Across from them are Jenkins and Machae. Next to me is Stevenson, across from him, Givvens. I stand first in line, right next to exit ramp. Across from me, Miranda is steady, her head titled back, eyes closed, breathing deep and with rhythm. As the tiny craft groans, lurches, and falls from the sky like a stone, she opens her eyes and looks at me, an inquisitive but lulling stare. The dull roar of the craft's landing boosters breaks the stillness and I feel the unique pressure of being stopped in a hurry. The craft touches down, the door falls open, and the eight of us swiftly undo the black straps, grab our weapons from their slots on the walls next to us, and step off into the deluged wasteland. We walk soaked and in silence for what feels like hours, though it takes us a mere 50 minutes or so to reach the center of the city.

I peer over the jagged ledge of a wall blasted down to its first ten layers of brick. Water pours out of the roiling slate-colored sky turning dirt to mud. My eyes canvas what used to be a courtyard, the cracked and tattered remnants of a fountain midway. I can see it spewing and churning crystal clear water, surrounded by even-cut deep green grass and young trees, people talking, eating ice cream, children running and playing. The sluggish squash of my comrade's boots behind me melts the placid image and makes me turn my head slightly, but my eyes remain fixed. I reach around my right arm, un-sling my rifle, and tuck it against my left shoulder, resting the barrel on the scraggy outcrop. Miranda's scratchy carrying whisper slits and blends into the gravelly barrage of raindrops.

"I smell an ambush."

"What's it smell like L-T?" Machae breaks in.

"It smells like my foot after I pull it out of your ass. Pay attention! Givvens, take Wheatly and Christiansen over to the left and through that busted doorway. Be quick. Stevenson, take Jenkins and Machae and deploy the Mark Six over to the right, next to that ledge for cover. Magnusun and I will deploy frags, then lay down suppressing fire. Givvens, when you see Stevenson's team open fire, advance up the left side. We'll follow you up the middle. Everyone got that?"

I didn't have to look to see everyone nodding their heads with intent. I nod too. A slow squash in the distance suddenly becomes hurried. I hear a muffled yell about thirty meters out. I sit up, brace, and aim down the barrel. The sound of displaced rocks draws my attention left. Two figures emerge from behind the side of half a small apartment, using it for cover, making hand signals and scanning about. They don't notice the grime-covered window just in front of them. I take a deep breath out and do what I was trained to do. I squeeze the trigger in rapid succession, a half second stutter between, leaning on my left leg propped under me like a car jack. Bursts of searing hot plasma, burning blue like the core of a giant star streak across the wasteland, crash through the glass, and take the entire right ribcage off the second of the two. His partner yells, 'Over here! Over here! 30 meters, dead ahead!'

The incontestable flunk of mortars resounds. I can't see where they're coming from. They whistle as if merry as they descend upon us, then thwack into the ground, blasting out shards of brick and wood and bits of steel; I duck under the ledge and crunch into a ball, debris decanting over me. Givvens' team moves across the alley towards the door, around the scorched wreckage of a car. Suddenly, machine gun fire rises above the clamor and dozens, hundreds of sharp pangs, shrill cracks and thick thuds permeate their sorry excuse for cover. I pop my head up to get a quick look and see no less than 50 soldiers scrambling out from behind piles of rubble and gaping sides of buildings, yelling and discharging their dated but no less deadly weapons wildly. The mortars stop. Miranda, now just behind me and firing shouts, "Grenades!" All eight of us pull one from our belts, smack the large black button atop them, and arch them towards our enemy. Two, three, five, seven, eight powerful explosions accompanied and followed by lancinating screams. The machine gun fire ceases, waiting for the smoke to clear, draping an eerie quiet save for distant moans of pain. This gives Stevenson's team time to deploy. I crouch and lean out to my right to see Machae smacking the top of the five and a half foot long weapon into its tripod. I wish I could have seen those vibrant eyes one last time.

A tearing zip; Machae looks down at his chest and falls back limp, lifeless into the muck. Stevenson yells, "Machae! Jenkins, pull him back, I'll cover you!" He lifts the massive weapon by himself and plants it down on a higher part of ground behind their cover, then squeezes hard on the dual triggers, his hands clenched airtight around the chrome handles. With a rapid booming thunk like too much bass through too small a speaker, streams of crackling cations charge out, a horde of animals fleeing an earthquake, stampeding, smashing and trampling everything in their path. What was left of someone's home blows into chunks and collapses in on itself. Stevenson turns in the directions of the mortar and machine gun fire, vigorously swiveling the weapon, each shot like a small grenade. Givvens and his team stand up from behind the car and open fire. Givvens yells something to his team, then slides off to the left, shooting as he moves. The mortar fire intensifies, trying to scare us behind our cover and give their soldiers a window to charge. Wheatly and Christiansen furiously spray the landscape, firing a three or five shot burst, then quickly snapping the barrel a foot or so left, then right, then left again, seeking anything moving, permeating the killing field with their outpouring.

An enemy springs from behind cover and is instantly slapped in the face with a round, taking his head off. Another tries to run for higher ground only to have his lungs plastered with blood against the wall in front of him. I rise to standing and push a small green button on my weapon, making it fully automatic. I pull and hold the trigger hard screaming, "Yeah! Yeah! Come on you motherfuckers, come on! Lay it on 'em boys!" The chug of my weapon, like an oncoming steam-engine train, drowns all other sounds around me and for those few dragging seconds I feel like Zeus himself, hurling thunderbolts at blasphemers. Wheatly tosses another grenade and Jenkins launches two at once, their reverberating blasts melding with the hundreds of zipping whining chugging and thudding spheres of shining death. Miranda shouts, "Cease fire, cease fire! Cease fi- hold your fire goddammit, hold your fire!"

It's quiet again. Plumes of rust-colored smoke swirl into the sky, dissipated by a breeze I don't feel. The downpour withers to a light shower. I look up at the whitening clouds coursing crossways with haste. I look down at my weapon, the crimson red bar on its side pulsing with urgency. I push down on the switch below it and the soda can-sized silvery power pack drops out. I reach behind my back to my belt, load up another, flick the switch back, and wait anxiously for the red light to turn green as the echoing shriek of it charging breaks the silence. I hear a half dozen more shrieks. A broad amber sunray, a spotlight illuminating the battlefield, suddenly splits the dreary grey. The clouds swiftly part, the rain dwindles to a trickle, and I hear the rising battle cry of a full company…no…a battalion of soldiers. It may as well have been ten thousand. My chest tightens; my lips chafe and crack from the thick, dry air rhythmically spewing from my mouth. My hands tremble and sweat onto my weapon until it nearly hydroplanes out of them. But my eyes remain fixed.

20 soldiers slither out from the rubble and into view, then 50, then 100. I take a deep breathe out. I switch my weapon to manual and take careful aim, firmly squeezing the trigger, one pull at a time, shooting for their sternums or stomachs. One down, three down, five down. Christiansen and Wheatly follow my lead firing solitary, well-placed shots, hitting their targets every time, suppressing not just the onslaught, but the fear, forestalling our most palling enemy: panic. Stevenson's

savage but calculated attack keeps the enemy from advancing too quickly and Miranda coordinately launches grenades into their ranks, intelligently timed and placed so that at no point could they mass into a group large enough to reach our line. Stevenson locks in the last Mark Six power pack. Miranda tosses our second-to-last grenade, leaving me with one. 200 more enemies swarm towards us, shouting and showering our cover with bullets. Miranda pulls out her short-wave transmitter, a small earpiece with a two-inch boom, and screams into it, alternating between demanding reinforcements and switching channels in search of Givvens.

"Sector 4-8-2, about 1,000 meters from the target, we are under heavy fire-"

An enemy grenade explodes not 10 meters from us, spewing dirt and stone and metal, in case they needed proof.

"We've got a man down and one MIA, we're low on ammo and are severely outnumbered, we need assistance, do you copy, over!?"

The radio pops and gargles, barely audible through the din of battle. *Reinfor…en-route…thirty mints…hold posishhhh-* Hold position. Sure. No problem.

"Givvens! Corporal Givvens, what is your position, over? Givvens, where the hell are you, get where I can see you goddammit! Givvens, do you copy?"

No answer. I turn to Miranda, prepared but terrified.

"L-T we can't stay here!"

A dozen rounds riddle the wall to my right, ripping bits off that smack into my face. I turn to shoot but catch the gleam of something, far in the distance. I shift my body left and squint; a zip like the one I heard before Machae was hit takes a chunk off the wall next to me, missing my chest by centimeters. "Sniper!" I call out. I never would have seen him had it not been for the sun. We crouch and tuck in our limbs. Miranda throws a smoke canister, almost lazily, over our heads. Within seconds, no one can see 5 meters in front of them.

"We're all about to run out of ammo, when the Mark Six is done so are we, what're we gonna use fucking rocks?"

"You hold this position for as long as you can Magnusun. I'm gonna go find Givvens. When Stevenson is out of ammo, cover his and Jenkins retreat to the southeast, then follow. Have Wheatly and Christiansen pan out to the west. We need to try and get around this force. We've still got a job to do. Set your transmitter to channel 4 and listen for priority messages from command. Otherwise stay off it. You're in charge Sergeant."

"Sure thing L-T."

I gulp hard enough to have swallowed my tongue and quickly scramble off to the right, switching between a low slow-paced crouch and an upright sprint, diving and sliding into the Mark Six's tripod, nearly knocking it over. Stevenson chides.

"Magnusun, what the fuck are you trying to do!? And why'd you pop smoke, I can't shoot what I can't see!"

"Shut up and listen."

Several grenades punch through the thick smoke but fall short, their blasts splashing dust and dirt and scraps of rubble over us. We squeeze our eyes closed and cover our heads with our arms. They know what they're doing; the smoke begins to clear.

"Listen to me, the Lieutenant is trying to find Givvens and we're running out of ammo. Reinforcements are on the way, but -"

20 enemy soldiers rush towards us. Stevenson shifts from intently listening to intently yelling, pumping out rounds, taking off arms, legs, heads, splattering blood like paint onto the ground. I fire anywhere he misses, the both of us ducking and swaying, making them take that extra half-second to aim. Another large group charges at Wheatly and Christiansen; they each pull the last grenade off their belts and halt the assault with them.

"But it's gonna take at least a half hour to get here. We're holding till the Mark Six is spent, then we gotta switch to our pistols to save rifle ammo, swing around the edges of these guys, and head to our target. Grab their weapons if you can get to 'em. You me and Jenkins will fall back to the southeast about 200 meters, then head north. Wheatly and Christiansen will move out to the west."

"What about Machae?"

"We'll come back for him when our re-up gets here, alright? Jenkins, you get all that?"

Jenkins stands cemented; he fires a shot per second picking off any soldier that pauses to aim before they can shoot, with nary a miss. His voice quivers as he responds.

"Sir, yes sir, but what about Givvens and the Lieutenant?"

"They'll have to take care of each other for now, all five of us go after them and ain't none of us goin' home. Jenkins, get on your transmitter and relay the orders to Wheatly, tell them not to call us, we'll call them. Stevenson, when you see him and Christiansen break off, that's when you go, then you Jenkins. I'll cover you two and follow, then blackout your transmitters until I say otherwise."

Jenkins nervously nods his head, relays the orders and goes back to shooting. Stevenson, still blasting away, yells back at me.

"What about this thing?" nodding at the veracious Mark Six.

"Leave it. No wait…fix a grenade to it, near the power pack. What's its charge level at?"

Stevenson looks at the bright red digital display on the top of the weapon.

"24 percent."

"Wait till it gets to 10. I'll pop it as we retreat. Either of you have any grenades left?"

Stevenson shakes his head. Jenkins doesn't respond.

"Fuck. Here…my last one."

"You're a genius."

"Watch it, more coming."

I take Jenkins lead, waiting for an enemy to aim and beating them to the punch. Stevenson slows his fire, waiting for the magic number. The battlefield is littered with bodies. The enemy advances in waves, replacing each soldier we kill with 3 more. Our cover is all but exhausted, blasted down to nearly nothing. I glance over to see Wheatly swatting Christiansen's arm; the two sling their rifles over their shoulders, pull out their pistols, and make an orderly withdrawal out of sight, the archaic snap and crack of their last resort weapons echoing into the distance, overpowered by the automatic spit of the guns of dozens of charging enemies.

"Time to go. Stevenson, fix that grenade. Jenkins, move Machae's body behind that wall over there, grab his ammo, then get going."

I switch my weapon back to automatic, load up my last power pack, and expend its charge in a frantic rage, unconscious of whether or not I'm hitting anything, the godlike sensation now more distant to me than the air in Machae's lungs. I look at his body, at the tennis ball-sized hole in his chest, cringe, and force back my tears. I glance down to see Stevenson wrapping black tape around the Mark Six and the grenade, then clamber off into a sprint. Turning slightly, I see Jenkins bounding over a mound of rubble. I pull out the one smoke grenade I decided to take and roll it to the Mark Six. I back away slowly, but stop and scan the landscape as I hear the spit and tear of distant gunfire from the direction that Givvens and Miranda had disappeared into. Stevenson calls from behind me, "What're you linin' up a picture, let's go!" I try to turn and hurry off but my eyes remain fixed. I wonder if I'd ever see Wheatly and Christiansen again. I wonder if I can lead what was left of my team to the caverns and back. I wonder if Miranda and Givvens are all right, if they would ever find each other. I get about halfway to Stevenson, kneel down, draw my pistol, aim at the dark green sphere attached to the Mark Six, and wait. I can barely see it through the smoke, but the contrast of the white barrel and the black tape make it stand out. A mass of soldiers plods forward, aiming and firing at me from the smoke as they pass through it, their bodies pushing it off like ghosts emerging from the nether.

I let loose a single shot, hitting the grenade that ignites the power pack into a massive glowing dome of seething blue and white luminance. A cacophonous clack precedes a shockwave of energy that knocks me flat on my back. I lay staring at the saffron sky for what seems like long enough to have lived a different life, my ears deafened and ringing, my muscles aching, my eyes glazed. Stevenson and Jenkins' strong hands pull me back and stand me up. I had no idea a Mark Six power pack would do that. Its construction was classified, even to us. Now I knew why. At least Machae can rest in peace. The three of us stammer off behind piles of stone and steel into uncertainty.

Part II

"Givvens...Givvens do you copy, over? Givvens, stop fucking with me, I know you're out here. If you're getting this but you can't give away your position, tap the mic twice..."

Two soft taps, the second louder than the first, put a smile on my face.

"Okay stay where you are, I *will* find you."

I sank low and kept close to the shambled walls, my body gradually vanishing in the fading light of the sun as it sank low and kept close to the wisps of clouds casting long and louring shadows over the embattled landscape. The combination of dust devils and the gauzy sheen of dusk trying to push its frail light through the cracks, the crevasses, and the swirling dirt rendered me all but invisible in my dark brown and black camouflage. The distant echoes of tumbling rocks being kicked and pushed by enemy search parties made me anxious, but not afraid. I stopped every dozen meters or so to look around, checking for scouts, snipers, and anyone else that could give away my position. The one that killed Machae was still out there somewhere, and I was determined not to be his next victim. My radio crackled and shrieked. Yelling and gunfire filtered though. Someone on Magnusun's team must have turned it on by accident. The echo of tumbling and scraping rocks intensified and without wasting another moment I ripped the transmitter from my belt and tossed it as far as I could. At the clack of it hitting the ground I moved up, but didn't get more than 10 meters before a pale white hand rose from the shaded rubble motioning for me to stop and get down. Just as I did, an enemy patrol, 15 soldiers at least, came up and over a mound of broken stone and twisted metal, guns drawn. They fanned out, looking every which way, attentive and poised. Givvens and I lay perfectly still, breathing slow and deep, our eyes closed, weapons tucked underneath us. The guards called to each other.

"You see anything? Thought I heard something over here…"

"Nah nothing over here, how about you?"

"We ain't gonna find shit here man, you saw that explosion. Probably took out half the damn south sector, nobody got out of that."

"Trust me private, she got out. Keep looking."

They were only looking for me? I could hear the crunch and scrape of boots drawing nearer until I felt the dust from the footsteps on the side of my face. I wanted to spring up and break a couple of necks, knife a couple of backs, and shoot a half dozen faces, but I didn't want to put Givvens at risk. He would almost certainly follow my lead and would almost certainly get shot. I waited, motionless and patient as the patrol passed, breaking off into pairs and disappearing into the rubble. Givvens sat up and leaned his back against a broken wall. I rose and slowly walked towards him. Givvens smirked and chuckled.

"Well that was about as close as shit can get, right Lieutenant?"

"I've been closer. Look, what's the idea of you goin off by yourself and not telling anyone where you were or why you couldn't complete the flanking maneuver?"

"Well, to answer the last question first, I got pinned down by that heavy machine gun and then a mortar landed practically right next to me. There was enough rubble around me to block the shrapnel, but it still knocked me on my ass and half covered me in dirt. When I came to, I saw some soldiers running past me and figured I would play dead until the coast looked clear. I couldn't see you guys from where I was so I just moved up on my own. Then I saw that explosion and decided to stay put."

"Not the worst thing you could've done. Anyway, we gotta move. Jason – I mean Magnusun, Jenkins, and Stevenson are making their way towards the objective along the east edge of the region. We've gotta meet them on this side and pincer the encampment at the tunnel entrance."

"Retreating not an option here I'm guessing?"

"Even if we tried I'm sure they're monitoring all the short-wave frequencies out here, they'd zero in on us before evac showed up. We were supposed to get reinforcements about twenty minutes ago, so either they can't find us or they're all dead. No, it's the caverns or nothing."

"Alright then, lead the way Lieutenant."

We quickened our pace confident that most of their attention was focused on Magnusun's team. I dropped my nearly empty plasma rifle and picked up a solid-round AR from the dead body of an enemy soldier. Givvens found a ten-gauge shotgun and several pin-and-lever grenades. The echoing cracks of gunfire grew louder and louder as we neared our objective. Soon we could see soldiers running off to the east, leaving less and less soldiers at the encampment near the caverns, which was now no more than a hundred meters away. I ran forward towards a raised section of rubble and cautiously looked over a jagged window base. Givvens followed and as he neared I gave my orders.

"Your radio still functional?"

"Yes L-T."

"Try the three of them, Magnusun first, someone has their radio on. If and when you get them, tell them to push forward to the caverns, then set up a defensive position wherever looks best. I'll come around to them."

"Come around…wait, what're you gonna do?"

"Sweep and clean."

"By yourself?"

"That wasn't a request Corporal."

"Yes L-T."

"Once they're set up, toss in a couple grenades to shake 'em up, then I'll know Magnusun's team is in position and finish my sweep. When I'm with them and you see us all move in together, you move up, you get all that?"

"Every word."

"Good luck."

I placed the assault rifle's strap over my head and swung the weapon around to my back with my right hand. At the same time I reached to my belt with my left hand and pulled a bright sliver 9½ inch blade, teethed on one side about halfway down, made of an experimental metal composite whose constitution was classified, even to me. I grasped the coarse black handle and flipped it in my hand so the tip pointed out and down. Givvens readied a grenade, pulling the pin, but keeping the lever firmly pressed against the casing. He called into the radio several times but got no response from Jason and his team. The gunfire from the east was no longer an echo, and we could see the faint blue glow of plasma rifle fire reflecting off the tainted windows and the pieces of stone burned nearly into glass from battles long forgotten. In the deepening dark, it seemed as if the city were alive again, the sound of footsteps, the light, the voices. I ran off toward the firefight.

From the west, 3 soldiers rushed Givven's position. I had to decide if I wanted to let him try and handle them and press on, or turn back and cover him. It would be easier for me to just ignore them but I already lost one of my soldiers. I wasn't going to lose another. Not today. I pivoted on the ball of my foot and spun myself around, barely losing any speed as I ran at the back of one the 3 soldiers. My knife gleamed for an instant as he turned just in time for me to thrust into his stomach and push him with me, using him as a shield. The other two soldiers fired aimlessly into his back. When I was close enough, I flung the body aside and in one fluid motion, like a dance I somehow already knew the steps to, slashed open the neck of the soldier on the left, and then spun around, kicked the gun out of the other soldier's hand, and stabbed diagonally downward into his chest. Two more soldiers ran out from the tunnel entrance and one immediately pulled a grenade from his belt and tossed it at me. He hadn't waited, however, for the fuse to burn, and I caught the grenade with one hand and threw it back at him.

The second soldier dove away and took cover behind a small pile of rocks and weapon crates just in time to hear his companion explode into bright red fleshy chunks. I brought my rifle to my side, ran to the tunnel entrance, and flipped over it on one hand, firing into the tunnel. Two thuds. The soldier that had taken cover was right next to me, too scared to move. I turned to him and he reacted, raising his weapon and squeezing hard on the trigger. The gun kicked up and I ducked down, the shots missing me entirely. I flicked my wrist and sent my knife zipping through the air and into the center of the soldier's chest. He gasped and fell over and as he did I ran up, yanked the knife from his body and tumbled forward under the gunfire of several soldiers retreating from Jason's position. I rolled up to one knee and with calm precision, firing short controlled bursts at the soldiers, killed two and forced the others to dive to the ground for cover.

Stevenson, light machine gun in hand, came charging through the rubble like a rhino, spraying the prone enemies and pin-cushioning them with rounds. Jason and Jenkins followed, each covering a flank, carefully aiming and shooting at the remainder of the disoriented soldiers. Stevenson flashed a huge almost wicked grin.

"Well, fancy meeting you here! I really thought we were gonna have some trouble getting up here but ya know, once these fuckers didn't outnumber us 20 to 1, they didn't put up much of a fight."

"Glad to hear it Corporal. Jason." I nodded at Jason, my eyes avoiding contact with his.

"Stevenson, do me a favor and wave Givvens over; he's on that ridge to the west. I need to sit down."

I sat right where I was, crossed my legs, put my hands over my knees, and breathed out hard enough to swirl some of the dirt in front of me. Stevenson motioned for Givvens; he jogged haphazardly toward the rest of us, the active grenade still clenched in his hand. Jason smiled at the sight of his friend.

"You son of a bitch, how they hell are you totally fine!? You should be fucking dead. It's good to see you man."

"I almost was!" Givvens yelled from a distance. "It's a good thing the Lieutenant here found me or who knows how long I'dve been out here."

"Love your choice of weapon!" Jenkins said, and then checked the display of his empty plasma rifle before tossing it aside.

Jason leaned in close and whispered to me, an elusive, complimenting sweetness to his voice.

"Somehow I knew you'd be okay…you still gave us quite a scare though. Don't leave us again okay?"

He threw his scavenged weapon over his shoulder and stuck out his hand to help me up. I didn't move. I didn't even look at him. Frozen in time, my heart racing, hands bloodied, sitting cross-legged in the dirt, for the first time in nearly ten years, I thought of home.

****

It was a dim afternoon in early fall. The leaves were just beginning to change, their gold's and red's mixing with the bold green grass into a perfect meld of otherwise unmatchable colors. The sky seemed cloudless but there was a sheer white overcast that broke the setting sun's rays into a blanketing fan and stretched them to the opposite horizon. I stood with my hand against a tall old pine tree and felt the stiff, grating bark pressing against my skin. It was almost painful but I was too focused on the doe that was warily approaching the small pond at the edge of my family's land, close enough to see how much bigger she was than me. The doe took a few steps then stopped to look around, then took a few more, her ears flipping and turning every which way, catching far off sounds I could only imagine.

She reached the pond, dipped her head down, and lapped up the cool water with her tongue, making tiny rhythmic ripples that slowly reached me and made the cattails sway. As I watched, I began to feel sad, but I couldn't figure out why. Perhaps I felt she was lonely, or that she was too anxious for no good reason. Perhaps it was how fragile the doe seemed, how exposed, as if anything that were to disturb the tranquil image would be as a brick smashing a stained glass window. Instinctively I took a step forward, wanting to get closer and as soon as I moved, the doe's head whipped up and her eyes and ears fixed directly on me. I froze, but after a second she ran off. I stood there staring at the tall grass she had made her exit through for some time. I wanted her to come back, to be comfortable in my presence, calm and unafraid. So much did I want to project this aura it angered me that I couldn't. My anger precluded any possibility of having such an air about me. I didn't really understand then, but I was setting myself up to fail.

"Miranda! Dinner's ready! Come on inside!" My mother called from the house. Really, she didn't have to yell. There was nothing between the house and the old pine tree to block the sound. Such open space carried noises on the wind like feathers. It's no wonder the doe could hear the rustling of rabbits in the brush or the stirring of birds in branches. I turned and ran to the house. A simple two-story humble abode, its cream-tan paint and black-shilling roof always seemed to fit snuggly in the brown and green of nature that surrounded it, even if it looked terrible in the pictures my father took to show his friends all the work he had done on it. All by himself he had added (and painted) a full-sized den on the left, a second floor porch, and built a garage on its right, big enough to hold two cars and that boat he always wanted, but never got. I reached the screen door and pulled it open.

"What were you doing out there all afternoon?" my mother asked.

"Nothin'. Just watchin' the animals and walkin' around 'n stuff."

"Well it's getting colder out there now, you should take some kind of jacket with you next time or you'll get yourself sick."

"I know mom. Thanks."

"Food's on the table, you help yourself."

Her apron was stained with all manner of spices and sauces, mostly wiped from her hands. She was the kind of cook that liked to feel the food, taste-test it every two minutes, and was always adding something to give body or flavor or intensity. She had a workingwoman's hands though; thick long fingers, rough palms, and a powerful grip. She carried herself with an upright posture that made her seem much taller than she actually was, and had an almost mechanical way of moving about the kitchen that more closely resembled a frantically busy secretary than a cook. She often wore her hair in tight curls that rested gently on her shoulders, the bobs like corkscrews dipped in honey. But she carried a heavy load that pressed on her and came through her eyes as if a dammed lake, the concrete slowly cracking. She did her best to hide it, but it was perhaps that very effort which betrayed the tiredness of her heart. My father, a burly broad-chested tower of a man, with a thick brown beard, had already finished eating and was leaned back in his chair with a newspaper in his face. I sat down and served myself a few slices of turkey breast, cranberry sauce, and a heap of garlic mashed potatoes that steamed as I mixed them with my mother's famous gravy. It smelled of basil and paprika and it poured like syrup. Just as I was about to eat my first fork full, my father spoke, his voice rough and resonating.

"So, yud rather eat rations half-made uh chemicals instead a that, and sleep in a three-foot wide cot instead uh yer own room?"

"Ernest, Jesus Christ, let her eat first would you?"

"She doesn't have ta say nothin'. It was a rhetorical question anyways, she ain't got no good answer."

"Nothing good enough for you I suppose."

"Now see ats what I'm talkin' bout, she ain't never got nothin' intelligent ta say, just smart ass one-liners she thinks'll jus make everybody shut up."

"That's not fair Ern, she's a young woman and she's allowed to have her own opinion and make her own decisions."

"Well ya got the young part right Mary, young is defnitly what she is, too young ta go off killin people."

"Dad, that's not the point okay, I need money for college, I know how tight you guys are, there's no reason for me to lose myself in a university for six years and stack up nine hundred thousand dollars in loans when I don't even know what I wanna do with my life yet."

"All the more reason fer you ta stay right here till ya figure that out."

"It's just two years dad! Two years and I'll have two hundred grand and a military service record that'll guarantee I get into any school I want."

"Well ya shouldn't a fucked up yer grades so bad yer last two years at Woodcrest, then you wouldn't have ta use dis as a excuse not ta show them universities yer transcript!"

"Yeah dad, that's exactly what it is…you got it exactly right."

"Don't git sarcastic wit me now, say what you mean or-"

"Or don't say nothin at all. Right. I'm not hungry anymore."

I pushed myself away from the table with one swift shove, turned and flung the screen door open and went back outside. I walked around to the side of the house and planted myself on a large rock jutting out of the ground. I peered over my shoulder through the half-open kitchen window. My mom stood with her hands balled in fists on her hips, her head cocked to the side. My dad shook his newspaper and brought it back to his face without a word.

"You know it's the same argument every time. Maybe if you tried bringing it up in a different way you might get a different response."

"Ain't no other way ta bring it up Mary! What she's doin is a foolish thing, she has no idea what she's gettin herself into.

My grandpa served in Iraq and Afghanistan, his daddy served in Vietnam and both a them'd tell you that war is no place for *anybody*, much less a Iowa-raised sixteen year-old little bit of a girl dats seen about as much of the world as a little ant in the dirt!"

"But there's no war right now, and there's not gonna be a war in two years. Nobody wants to fight, you've seen the headlines. You're reading them right now, "*Great Britain brings middle east expeditionary forces home, France pulls troops out of Mail, U.S. leaves Israel and Palestine to their own devices, North Korea reestablishes non-aggression pact with the South, China dry-docks pacific fleet*". Everyone's turning inward, trying to fix their own problems, lord knows we've all got about as much as we can handle. They say there's only enough oil left to last another 15 years, who's gonna go to war when they can't even be sure they can gas up their tanks and airplanes?"

"That's jus the thing bout wars. They just happen, oft' times when yer least expectin it. Some poor dishonored fool goes off 'n caps some other fool in a suit on a podium and the next thing ya know there's picket lines and riots, there's drafts, and then the guns come out and they send everybody they can. And thats the outa-the-blue example, what makes you think China or North Korea, or even Russia isn't gonna make a last minute push ta grab n' horde as much oil as they can?"

"Maybe Miranda won't have to go. Maybe they'll keep her here, or give her a job away from the frontlines or something, somewhere it's not all about killing."

"War's all about killin, ain't nothin' else to it. There ain't no reason for her ta go anywhere near a gun, much less near someone else who has one, who's not gonna hesitate for one second to-"

"Ernest, please, okay. I know what you're saying but I've tried to talk her out of it too and she really just thinks it's the best thing for her, for her future. It's about that time we start letting her make these kind of grown-up decisions and let her learn from the consequences."

"She ain't gonna learn shit if she's dead."

"Earnest!"

"You think I'm jus sayin that for the effect of it!? I love her too Mary, an I don't wanna see her name jammed in on some list er scratched up on some wall wit a whole bunch uh other faceless nobodies cause she thought she needed a head start!"

"So what would you have her do!? Stay here for the rest of her life, in this no-name town, in the middle of nowhere, with two friends, a dead-end job, and a completely disenchanted outlook on life? You're the one always building shit around here! You of all people should know what it feels like to accomplish something all on your own!"

"That's different!"

"How!? How is it different, you tell me!"

I returned my gaze to the setting sun, my willpower forcing my mind to wander. I wondered what my parents would do if

I left, right then and there, and never came back. It would be easy to get lost in such a big world, and I knew no one would ask questions, not a volunteer. People always said that volunteers make the best soldiers. I had never understood why but seeing my parents scream at each other over me made me think that maybe it was because those volunteers had something they wanted to leave behind. Something they didn't want to have to deal with, or even remember. That by throwing themselves head first into the service, they would be stripped clean of everything that had made them who they were before and come out the other side a different person. Stronger, smarter, braver, more aware. Really I didn't want any of that. All I wanted was to make a difference; to have connections with people that actually meant something, bonds not easily broken. I wanted to matter. At least that's what it had started out to be. My mother's voice calling my name suddenly changed to Jason's and as I was pulled out of my memory I realized that the only difference I had made up to now was to reduce the surplus population. I had killed more enemies than I could count, and watched more comrades die than I wanted to recall. I shivered slightly as if snapped out of hypnotism and stared up at Jason with fearful eyes. Tears welled up, but the puzzled look on Jason's face forced them back. I pressed my eyes closed, shook my head, and when I looked back at him, all that remained was Lieutenant Miranda Merridan, Spec Ops division Delta, CQC specialist, and commanding officer of 1st platoon.

"You alright Miran – I mean, Lieutenant?"

"I'm alright Jason. Just a little shook up is all."

Givvens came stumbling into the semicircle the team had formed around me as I took Jason's hand and stood.

"Man, did you see that? I mean, *did you fucking **see** that!?*"

"See what?" Jenkins asked plainly.

"The Lieutenant, she was all like super ninja kung-fu fighting knife swiping death goddess and shit! She killed like ten, twelve dudes just back to back without even stopping to take cover or nothin! Unbelievable!"

"It wasn't all that. I just did what I had to do to keep my team safe. I failed once already, I'm not going to fail again."

Stevenson let out a hardy sarcastic laugh.

"You didn't fail a damn thing Lieutenant, that was a bullshit situation. We're lucky you were here to tell us what to do, otherwise we'd be way back there still, and not breathin' lemme tell you."

"We really walked right into that ambush didn't we. It's almost too convenient, ya know?"

Givven's question didn't have the impact he intended. Stevenson shrugged his shoulders, Jason shook his head, and Jenkins was watching our flanks for stragglers. I rose to my feet and stared down the tunnel entrance, looking long and hard, half expecting some terrible monster to come screeching out of it.

"Givvens, toss that grenade in there, would you?"

The stifled bang of the explosive vibrated the dirt above the entrance and clanking metal could be heard from farther inside.

"Well there *was* a door in our way!" Stevenson joked.

"Looks like Wheatly and Christiansen aren't coming" Jenkins said sadly.

"We can't wait for them" I replied flatly.

Jason breathed out a heavy sigh.

"So how do we proceed?"

"Very carefully", I said in the most serious tone I could. "And very slowly; by the numbers. Check all the corners, all the doorways, and all the sub-chambers one at a time until we reach the control room. Get your thermo-visors on. Jenkins, you're on map detail. Stevenson, you bring up the rear. I'll take point."

We filed into the tunnel, swallowed by the haunting darkness.

Part III

I wanted to move but couldn't, frozen by the tension of the moment. My concern for Jason preempted all my instincts and experience and I couldn't understand why. Nothing like this had ever happened to me before. At the same time I trusted his skill and was almost curious to see how he would handle this. He stood staring down at a screen on a computer console as the guard, in shock at first, did nothing. Jason heard him start to reach around his back for the assault rifle slung over his shoulder. He dropped to one knee and with the speed of a wild west gunslinger, drew his pistol and hit the guard square in the chest. He gasped and collapsed, but the guard had managed to get the rifle into his hands and he squeezed the trigger as he fell, firing off a burst of rounds that echoed far into the caverns, the sound reverberating through the narrow metal corridors as if the bullets themselves had ricocheted off them. It was not the gunfire but the distant shouts and the rustle of soldiers moving with haste that snapped me out of my trance.

"Jason! The fuck is wrong with you, get back here!"

"Damn it, sorry, just-just cover me for one second!"

Jason whipped his tablet out from his front jacket pocket and stuck it in the connector slot to the left of the screen, then pressed a button on the console.

"Jason, I hope this is more important than your life because…"

"It might be."

"Hurry!"

"Okay…okay, done!"

Jason snatched the tablet out of the slot and rushed behind the thick steel pillar I was posted up against as I slapped a fresh clip into my rifle and snapped the lever back, loading the first round. Until this we had managed to remain undetected on our foray, making a couple of quiet kills and securing our flanks with professionalism. As we approached the central chamber, where the enemy base's command center resided, I had even hoped to plant the explosives and leave without a fight. In ten years of service I had never failed a mission. I couldn't have stood the disappointment and had completed the bulk of several missions on my own, after my entire team had been killed because what little intel that was provided had been wrong, or because advancing together made us too easy a target and I left them behind. I saw it all happening again. I could have told them to hold position and gone on my own; I would have been better off. I had done it many times before, and each time I left, none of them made it out alive. For years I had done nothing differently and had always accomplished my objective. I looked at Jason trying to appear unfazed but I could feel the fear emanating from him, pushing out through his tempered exterior. For a moment I saw a young boy, rifle half the size of his body, his mind overwhelmed with an impossible task that still he would see through, to whatever end. I knew he wasn't staying for himself. He was staying for us.

Maybe…for me. My voice shook slightly as I gave my orders.

"Okay…okay backtracking will take too long, we're gonna have to get out another way. Stevenson, take Jenkins and follow that corridor over to the right until you get to a T-section, then go right. According to the map there's an emergency ventilation shaft that leads to the surface. We'll hold 'em here, then you radio me and we'll follow you up but don't wait for us. If we don't make it, you blow the place."

I turned, detonator in hand, and tossed it to Stevenson. A low-pitched crackling thunk rang out and I cried out in pain. The detonator fell halfway between Stevenson and me, dead in the open. I slid down against the pillar clutching my left shoulder and trying to cover a hole big enough to stick my whole hand into. Eyes wide I panted and shivered, grunted and groaned, trying to keep my gun up. Stevenson shouted, "Lieutenant! Ah shit, Miranda, fuck *fuck* *fuck*!"

Automatic fire erupted from three directions, the bullets pinging and panging all around. Jason dove to the left, grabbed the leg of a nearby metal table and yanked it in front of him, in the same motion flipping it on its side and sliding it up next to the pillar. Givvens turned and fired at a pair of guards coming from a corridor just to the left of where we had entered, spraying madly into it. At the same time, Stevenson sprinted to me, sliding on his knees just beneath an intensifying hail of bullets. He wrapped his arm around my waist and pulled me behind the up-turned table, Jason laying down suppressing fire, trying to cover us. Jenkins was crouched behind a large steel desk he was slowly dragging, moving it behind the table and forming a makeshift bunker between the left wall, the pillar, the desk, and the table. Jenkins and Givvens leapt over the desk into the bunker and everyone crouched. Like stepping into our own coffins we were trapped, death's scythe ready to take our heads off should we raise them. Givvens yelled over the gunfire.

"All this way for nothing! This is such fuckin bullshit, I *knew* this was gonna happen!"

"They knew we were coming!" Jason said, shaking the tablet in his hand as he stuffed it back into his pocket.

Givven's spirit visibly sank as his face contorted in horror, then anger, then resolve. He rose and fired his weapon faster than I thought possible, unloading shell after shell, his screaming nearly overpowering the clack and thud of his shotgun and the piercing dings of the bullets being fired back at him. Stevenson followed and covered the opposite side. Jenkins peered over the desk behind us, looking for a way to escape without getting mowed down. Jason shifted over to me.

"L-T, what do we do!? What are your orders!? Miranda!"

My vision blurred and faded in and out. I felt dizzy, and the sounds of battle were but a distant hum. I wanted to just close my eyes and rest for a moment, but Jason's voice pushed through everything.

"NO! No, don't you die on me, don't you dare give up, you fight! We're not gonna die down here, not like this, you stay with me goddammit, stay with us!"

I looked at him as my eyes cleared slightly and my hearing began to fade back in. He lifted his thermo-visor and looked around frantically. His eyes caught something and he aimed his pistol and fired a single shot. The bullet hit its mark. Rotating blue lights dropped from the ceiling and a loud siren activated. Thick, ridged metal doors rose up from the floor at each of the entrances to the room and sealed it off. The gunfire stopped. A grenade came flying into the room just over the door at the far end of the room and bounced off the table. The team pressed their bodies flat on the ground and covered each other's heads, Jason pushing me over and covering my whole body with his. The explosion pushed the desk back a full meter at least and we were pushed with it. The shrapnel, flung out and up, stuck into the table's frame, piercing it, but not penetrating it. Stevenson breathed out a heavy sigh as he stood up.

"Okay…where's the detonator?" he asked sarcastically.

Jason stood and scanned the floor.

"In pieces."

"God…dammit!" Stevenson grunted as he punched the pillar.

"Was probably that damn grenade" Jason said pointing at the desk pin cushioned with shrapnel.

Jenkins cut in.

"Son-of-a-bitch. And we're all trapped down here, what the hell are we gonna do? Thanks a lot Magnusun."

"Hey, HEY! I did the first thing I could to keep several dozen guys with guns from surrounding and executing us!"

"Yeah, give 'em a break man" Givvens said in support.

Stevenson yelled and pointed his finger accusingly at Jason.

"Yeah well it's his fucking fault we got caught in the first place!"

Jason reached into his pocket and pulled out his tablet.

"Yeah, but the data that got us caught says that doesn't matter anyway because *they knew we were coming*!"

Jason flung the tablet at Stevenson like a frisbee. He caught it, turned on the screen and began paraphrasing aloud the section of info that stood out the most to him.

"Okay, huge transmission log uhhh…at 2:38 this morning this base intercepted a communication from Commander Tritium, that's our guy, to Commander…Brackard, I don't even know who that is…at the Nevada HQ detailing our mission. Seems harmless enough but…the frequency is listed as 44.82 at 26GHz."

"So. That's an encoded channel only the military can translate" Jenkins said matter-of-factly.

Jason responded.

"Exactly, but they didn't have to decode it. It was transcribed directly from the transmission to the log."

Stevenson looked up from the papers in disbelief. Givvens followed Jason's lead.

"Which means they must have a military decryption program running automatically, monitoring the frequencies."

Jason responded.

"Which means the military would immediately notice the distortion from the piggy-backed signal and change the frequency unless..."

"Unless they're letting them hear it."

Stevenson said, and the room fell silent. Jenkins sat on the ground where he was. Stevenson tossed the tablet back to Jason and leaned his back against the pillar. Givvens, still in the makeshift bunker, slumped to the floor, closed his eyes and tilted his head back until it rested on the top of the up-turned table. I cringed and grasped my shoulder, looking at my uniform for a good place to tear off a piece of it to use as a tourniquet, but there was no bleeding to stop. The wound had been cauterized by the shot; a shot that came from a high yield energy weapon, similar to our standard issue plasma rifles, but more powerful. It was a miracle it didn't take my arm off. The Black Hand weren't just getting information from the military; they were getting weaponry from them too. What were the chances we would run into a weapon like that here? Even if they had pulled it off a dead soldier, would they still have ammo for it? How would they even know how to use it? I had fought countless of Black Hand's and never once had I seen one with a weapon like ours. Jason reached into his right jacket pocket, took out a syringe of morphine, and jabbed it into my left bicep. The 5 of us milled, waiting for something, anything, to let us know what we should do. Stevenson examined the doors; Jenkins examined the computers, all of which were heavily encoded, locked down by the security systems Jason had activated when he destroyed the still smoking panel that saved our lives. Givvens paced back and forth, opening drawers and cabinets randomly, probably looking for weapons and ammo. Jason sat by my side with his arm around me, our hands entwined. I squeezed occasionally, clenching my teeth and squinting from the pain. At last my eyes focused completely and my ears popped and I was calm and coherent again.

"Is-is everyone okay?"

Jason smiled and Stevenson walked over.

"Are we okay? Fuck, are YOU okay!? Jesus Christ you scared the hell out of us."

"I'm alright. First time for everything I guess."

"You mean you've never been shot before?" Jenkins asked from halfway across the room.

"Never been injured before, at least not in battle. Guess my luck finally ran out."

"Yeah that'll teach you, haha!" Stevenson joked. I smirked and shook my head. Stevenson continued.

"By the way, did you catch anything of what happened? Cause in case you didn't, I'd like to be the first to let you know that the Neo United Nations has officially fucked us over in the worst possible fucking way. Or is it the best way…"

"Yeah I heard what I needed to. They set us up. We didn't stumble into that ambush back near our landing zone. It was waiting for us the whole time."

"Waiting right between the base and the LZ command changed us to at the last minute" Givvens added.

"So what do we do now?" Jenkins asked, approaching the group. Stevenson responded before I could.

"Well if we open the doors, we die. If we don't open the doors, we die. I for one would love to get them open and at least take some of these fuckers down with us before…"

Givvens interrupted, his voice full of zeal.

"No! One of us has to get to the surface. We can't let them keep doing this, who knows how many teams have been torn to pieces because our commanders have something else going on!"

"He's right. Otherwise Machae died for nothing." Jason said.

"Alright man, fuck, what do you suggest we do then?" Stevenson asked.

I answered softly, almost as if speaking to myself.

"Maybe I can hack the computer system, try and get only one of the doors open."

"You…can hack?" Stevenson asked in bewilderment.

"I can do a lot of things Corporal, otherwise I doubt I would have survived this long."

"The system is heavily coded, and has multiple password-locks and encryptions, I mean…" Jenkins said in a questioning tone.

"Well it seems to me that if they could get this place out of lockdown they would have done it by now, which means this room was designed to act as a last line of defense. They probably didn't expect us to make it this far. Or maybe they let us in here on purpose. I don't know. But either way I imagine it will take a while for them to get a hold of something big enough to blast those doors open. So we've got time, if nothing else."

Jason smiled brightly, comforted by my apparent confidence as I explained. In reality I didn't see much chance for us. Even if I could open just one door, what were the chances there wouldn't be a cadre of soldiers waiting just outside it? Could I take them? Yes. Would they kill most or all of my team while I dispatched them? Probably. I began drawing up scenarios in my head of how I might be able to avoid losing anyone else but they were fantasies, not real plausible solutions. Again the thought crossed my mind to get myself out and leave them here, returning for them when I thought I could lead them to safety, but that had never worked before and it wasn't going to work this time. No. I had to stay with them. Even if in the end none of us made it out, at least I would die knowing I did everything I could for the soldiers under my command this time, mission be damned.

Stevenson tossed his gun aside.

"Whatever you say Lieutenant. Anything we can do to help?"

"You and Givvens have the most direct training in computer system analysis, am I right?"

The two nodded their heads.

"Okay, each of you take a terminal opposite me and do exactly what I tell you, when I tell you. Jason could you…help me up?"

My voice shrank towards the end and my words trailed off. Jason put my right arm over his shoulders and gripped my left hand, which I made into a fist, from underneath. He reached around my waist from behind and tried to grab the back of my pants as we stood together, but his hand slipped and when he tried to grab it again, he got my ass cheek instead.

"Oh, sorry" Jason said timidly.

"No sweat" I said, completely monotone and devoid of emotion. Jason wasn't sure how to react. Then I whispered to him.

"You can grab it all you want if we get out of here in one piece."

I realized as I spoke the words that it was a childish thing to say, but the lid on my feelings was rattling from the pressure that had built up since before the mission had even begun and I felt as if I would explode if I didn't at least make a joke. I meant it as one, but I wasn't stupid. I knew it would stick in Jason's mind like a railroad spike. Part of me worried that it would cloud his instincts and slow his reactions; I was willing to take that chance. There was something deeper I wanted to get to in him. I knew the boy in his heart that was so clear to me before was falling in love with the girl in mine; he would use it as a catalyst to spur his mind and his body beyond what they normally might have been able to handle. It felt so silly to me, yet I knew that Jason wouldn't be truly fooled by the comical nature of my comment. I was giving him permission, saying that I wasn't blind to him; that I knew all along and that I wasn't going to let rank and uniform, or the threat of death get in the way of the only real connection I'd felt with another person since before I left home. After all it was possible, likely in fact, that none of us would make it out of this alive, and I wasn't going to die, or see Jason die, knowing that I should have said something to let him know that my feelings were not so far from his. Jason slowly moved his hand from my ass back to my waist and gripped my hand even tighter, as if to say 'Thank you. I thought I was alone in this'. You're not alone Jason, I thought to myself. And for the first time in as long as I could remember, neither was I.

I sat down in front of the command center's main control console, not much more than a giant screen angled so that it nearly faced the ceiling, projecting a virtual keyboard onto a space just below it. Stevenson and Givvens took their seats next to me, in front of two smaller but otherwise identical screens. They stretched and cracked their necks and knuckles. I tapped the screen to wake up the console and rapidly stroked a handful of virtual keys, a slight vibrating sensation from the console itself letting me know my touches had registered.

"Bypass the primary route code selector in the 16th communications grid" I calmly relayed to my team of untrained hackers.

Stevenson put his hand to his ear and said, "Do what, where, how?"

"I've already cracked the initial password and pulled up the communication's master file. Use the keyboard number pad's right arrow to scroll across the pages I have centered on everyone's screen until you get to the 16th." Jenkins and Stevenson tapped on the key as I continued.

"The first file at the top will read "Primary Route Code Selector". Hit enter then scroll down. The file will come with you. When you get to the bottom of the list," the two began scrolling down, "Hit enter again and the file will drop there. Press the key that has a symbol of what looks like a drop-down menu with a mouse pointer over it. It's just to the left of the left arrow key. A menu will pop up and the 4th item down from the top will read…"

"Refresh Procedure Priorities?" Givvens asked as he highlighted the option, several seconds ahead of Stevenson.

"Select that and a dialog box pops up requesting a password. I can't just overload this system's RAM to cause a permissions gap like I did with the entry-level password; this is going to take some work, but it's also the fun part, and the reason why I was having both of you, as separate guest users, doing the same thing at the same time. The point of hacking, at least when it comes to modern heavily encrypted military databases, is to trick the computer into thinking that every time a particular action is performed, it is performed for the first time, thus eliminating automatic security features designed to protect the system. No system will ever bar the user access on the first incorrect input. It's a fail-safe so General hot shit doesn't get locked out of his own defense grid because he had one too many and bumped the wrong key before he decided to pay the fuck attention."

The team gave a soft, tired, but nonetheless genuine swill of laughter.

"When two guest users try to access the network at the same time, the system, unable to reconcile this impossible dilemma of "how can the same human exist twice", silly computers, assumes that every re-attempt at access is a new user, so we get unlimited tries to find the password. The reason I had you move that file is because of a glitch within this system that stems from a memory accommodation miscalculation. In other words, whoever built this network didn't put the files in the proper ordering structure the last time they were modified, like ordering something by Date when the core operating system was designed to prioritize Name ordering. By moving that file, the entire ordering sub-structure is now confused, causing all code saved in files with the same previous ordering structure to become randomized. But since the file structure has only been reordered and not changed, the operating system remains functional, but nothing does what it would normally do. Number keys will turn to letters, escape to enter, page up to alternate, etcetera. While the password dialog box is open though, only letter and number keys will perform any action, so hitting a 4 that's become a delete won't do anything because it's not a letter or number. In short, all the command line prompts for the system have changed at the binary level. Now, find out which key is the space bar and avoid that."

The pair pressed key after key, quickly, but attentively, until each found what their respective space bar had become.

"From here, all you have to do is type a whole bunch of randomness because the password is just a bunch of randomized letters and numbers, filling the entire box because all spaces therein have been automatically replaced with another key. It takes about 3 to 4 seconds for the system to cross-check the password; each of you must press enter within this amount of time or the system will lock up. Shouldn't be hard as you really just need to type as fast as you can. I will be doing the same. This is why one needs a *team* of hackers. With one person, this would take days. With 3 it takes only hours. The more terminals the better. Unfortunately, this is all we've got to work with so let's hope those doors hold out. GO!"

The three of us struck furiously at the keys, making sure not to blanket them, and to spread out our pattern of typing, slowly shifting over and around, back over and down and up, producing similarly typed clumps and gaining as many permutations from as focused a set of variables as possible. It was a mathematical certainty we would find the password. But how long? We could get it on the first try, but realistically, 6 hours at least.

"If one of you gets tired, have Jason or Jenkins take your place for a bit. I know you guys can't type as fast."

"Not half as fast" Jenkins half-mumbled from the dreary, barely-lit far end of the room.

"But at least we can keep working."

"What about you Mir-ah-Ma'am, Lieutenant...L-T"

"I'll be fine. Keep an ear on that door would you?"

"Sure thing L-T."

Jason saluted, smiled, and walked over to the door that would lead to our freedom. Hours passed. Stevenson and Givvens switched off a few times. They were all exhausted to the point of stagnation. The typing slowed over time, each not confident they were even hitting different sets of keys in different patterns anymore. Just as it seemed there was no longer any point to what we were doing, the dimmed screens turned bright and the words "Access Granted" appeared in bold-face flashing green.

Stevenson yelled out, "Hey, shit, that's it, we got it...how the fuck did we do that?"

"With patience", I said. "Good job everyone. I'll take it from here."

I sat up in my seat, moved the chair closer to the terminal, and gave my knuckles a good cracking. I had all but forgotten about my wound as I started tapped the keys twice as fast as before; on-screen passed a blur of text and numbers and code, windows popping up and closing one after the other. A side-bar on the left began filling up with lines of code and scrolling down; then it started flashing.

"Jenkins, can you find me a flash-drive? There's bound to be one around here somewhere."

Jenkins started flipping over desk organizers and pulling open drawers, clawing everything out of them. After a few moments, I heard a plasticy smack on the floor and saw him kneel down and recover a small thin rectangle with tiny metal pins across the bottom on one end.

"Okay, see that slot just beneath and to the left of my left elbow?" I asked, still typing. "Stick it in there."

Jenkins did so and after another few seconds the side bar started emptying, the code flowing downward one line at a time. When it was empty, I snatched the flash drive out of its slot and walked briskly over to the rightmost door. I found a similar looking slot on a small control pad beside the door frame and clicked the drive into it. I took a few steps back and waited in nervous impatience. Everyone gathered behind me. A slight shudder, then a soft click, then a loud clank, and the door rolled down and open. No soldiers. Stevenson was the first to celebrate.

"Yes, *yes*, let's get the FUCK...outta here! Listen, Lieutenant, I don't know what the hell you did, but thank you. Thank you thank you thank you!"

"What do we do about the explosives, the base?" asked Jenkins.

Stevenson waved his hand in a dismissing fashion, "Leave it man, who cares, it doesn't even matter really, does it?"

I couldn't resist the chance.

"No. We still have to complete our mission."

Givvens jaw dropped open as he threw his hands out.

"Wha, Mira-...L-T I mean, come on! How, HOW are we gonna do that, why should we..."

"Maybe someone did set us up. But if it's true what I said before, and we were never meant to get this far, maybe destroying this place will stick a nice fat wrench into future operations. We don't know either way but no good could possibly come from leaving this place standing so I say we take it out. And I know just how to do it."

I walked back to the main computer and started typing like crazy again. The rest of the team watched in stunned silence. Jason spoke.

"What're you doing?"

"These explosives are temp-sensitive..."

"Meaniiiiiiiiiiiiiing…?" Stevenson goaded.

"If they get too cold, they shut down and become useless. If they get too hot they…who wants the bonus points?"

"Explode…" Jason said with a sly tone and a smirk of delight.

"Correct sir. I'm simply raising this room's temperature over the safety-locked maximum and cooking those things till they pop."

"Will you marry me?" Stevenson joked.

"Only if I get to bite your head off afterwards."

Stevenson raised an eyebrow in reconsideration and everyone chuckled. I finished typing then motioned to Jason for a firearm. He handed me his pistol and I emptied a clip into the computer.

"Okay, time to go."

Just as we moved toward the exit I heard the same shudder, click and clank that had preceded the opening of our escape route. Slowly the other three doors began to peel open. Givvens panicked.

"Wha-what the hell's going on, why are all the doors opening!?"

I gasped silently as my eyes bounced back and forth.

"Goddammit. The temp-override must have triggered a deep-level safety measure, we're about to have company. Let's move!"

We grabbed what weapons and ammo were left and ran for the exit. We followed the corridor down to the T-section and made a right, looking for the ventilation shaft. We reached it quickly, and just as quickly realized we had no effective way to climb up and out. I pulled my knife from my belt and stabbed it into the inside wall of the shaft.

"I hope everyone still has their knives cause that's your ticket out! I'll cover you, now go! Stevenson, you first."

Stevenson pulled out his knife and, reaching as high as he could, jammed it into the wall. He pulled himself up on it, placed his back on the opposite wall, and his feet across from him, barely reaching. As fast as he could, he pulled the knife out and jammed it higher up in the wall, then pressed his back against the wall and pulled on the handle, scooting up the wall at a disturbingly slow pace.

"This is gonna take forever" Jason said, peering up through the shaft, seeing how far away the light was.

"Even if you go one right after the other?" I asked.

"It's gotta be at least 15 meters to the surface, if you watch how Stevenson is going, it'll take him an hour, not including breaks. And he's the strongest guy here."

"Okay. So you just need a distraction to buy you some time, or even make them think you're somewhere else. Alright then. You're in charge, get everyone up there then go up yourself. If all those doors opened I can get back out the way we came in."

"Through all those Blank Hands!? You're out of your fucking mind, you're *hurt*, you should be going up that vent right now, hell I should carry you up there, you're gonna get yourself killed!"

Jason's voice was well beyond mere reasoning and falling full over into despaired concern. I felt only sorrow as I looked into Jason's fierce eyes. I knew he wanted to protect me, even from myself, from my own over-confidence. I wanted things to be different this time. I realized that I had survived all this time because I had only ever taken care of myself. Even when I left my teams behind to seek out the enemy and my objective on my own, I did it because they would have just got in my way. I used all of my training and all of my talent to create a no-win situation for my enemy, every time. Sometimes that had meant leaving my soldiers behind. Sometimes that meant putting them in harm's way to the point where, because of the disparity between my skill and that of my soldiers', it was a calculable certainty that they would not be able to survive the situation I had put them in, even though I would. Now I would do the opposite. I would put myself in harm's way; run straight into the jaws of death against impossible odds so that my team would be safe. I put my hand on Jason's shoulder, then leaned forward and kissed him deeply, putting all of myself into him for a few fleeting seconds.

"This is something I have to do Jason. It can't be any other way. I'm sorry." And in a flash, I slipped around a corner and was gone.

Part IV

I always thought Morgan was half crazy. But I didn't think he'd actually go through with it. He knew how mom and dad felt. They had talked about it, argued over it, even made stupid bets with each other. But in the end, it was Morgan's choice and it felt like he wanted to prove once and for all that he'd grown up. Morgan hardly ever called me. Either we happened to be in the same place at the same time, or we weren't. He never seemed to want to go even slightly out of his way to hang out. But there it was, the voicemail, from Big Bro, flashing on my phone, waiting to be heard. 'Meet me at my high rise, 6 o'clock, you know the room. See you later little bro.' That was all he said.

The door was unlocked and slightly ajar when I got there. I guessed he gave it a lazy push when he came in, never imagining anyone else would walk through. Perhaps he thought I wouldn't even come. Morgan stood by the triple pane body-length window overlooking the south end of the city, his hands clasped behind his back in true military 'at-ease' fashion. He didn't turn to look at me, but I knew he knew I was there. He pulled one of his usual's and started talking to me mid-thought.

"It's a funny thing. Isn't it?"

"What is?" I asked softly.

"Life is. You've got this idea in your head of who you wanna be. What you wanna do. And you might even be thinking, 'yeah, that's who I am, this is how I do shit.' But the reality is far from it. The way people see you and the things you do…it's totally different. Like you're someone else entirely."

"I don't know what you mean…"

I walked up almost parallel to my brother. He was nearly twice my size. Arms big around as water treatment pipes, massive chest, legs like tree trunks, and hands wide and strong enough to palm and crush a bowling ball. Or at least that's how I saw him, which made me suddenly understand what Morgan was saying. How we see things isn't always how they really are. I looked up at him, his eyes still fixed on the cityscape.

"But if people aren't seeing you how you see yourself, who's wrong? I mean, which is the real you?"

"HA, beats me. Guess that doesn't matter much now…"

I looked down at the floor, then up and out the window, wondering if Morgan was looking in the same place I was.

"Where they sending you?"

"Some island in the pacific, got some name I can't pronounce. That's for the regular grunt type stuff. Then it's Nevada for my 4 year spec. ops stretch. You know, if I make it."

"You will."

"Heh heh, yeah I hope so. I don't care much for the idea of being some random dude with a rifle, but being able to get all the juicy details of what's really going on, roll out with some real badasses, take the fight to the enemy's doorstep. That's my kinda show."

"Are you sure? I mean, that's really what you want the rest of your life to be about?"

Morgan turned to me, keeping his posture, and I looked back at him.

"Rest of my life, what, nah man it's just part of it. I ain't gonna be able to do that shit when I'm 40. After I serve my term, I retire, then I can do whatever the hell I want for as many years as I've been alive already, maybe more. But I ain't even worried about all that yet. Gotta survive to 40 first, ya know?"

My voice changed from casual banter to dim surrender. I knew there was no answer Morgan could give me for what I was about to ask that would satisfy me, but I had to ask anyway.

"Why Morgan? Why are you doing this? None of us want you to go but you're going anyway…why?"

"That's exactly why little bro. I'm gonna decide what's best for me, I'm gonna decide what to do with my life. And I'm gonna decide what's the best way I can help this dying world. Everyone tells me go left cause they seen what's over there and they know it's safe and they think it's right. Well then I'm gonna go right to find out what's over there, even if it's wrong. Just in my nature I guess."

"Come on, there's gotta be more to it than that. Or you don't wanna get into it cause you think I won't understand?"

"Nah, that's not it Jason, I know you're a smart kid, you got a good head on your shoulders. All the more reason for you to stay in school and not go off and do something crazy like I'm doin. No this path is just for me man, accept it or don't, but this is what I was meant for. I can feel it. And that's the best explanation I can give you. Even if you don't really understand now, you will someday. Believe me you will."

I returned my gaze to the city, one of the last untouched by the degradation that was spreading like a virus, tearing the life away from what was once a beautiful world, full of grandeur and promise. Now only a handful of sanctuaries remained, surrounded by conflict that was undetectable from where I was standing, yet seemed to be waiting just beyond the horizon, ready to rise up and wash over the buildings and sweep away all that I loved. And here was my big brother, riding out on his steed of courage and stubbornness to meet that rising tide. A seemingly futile effort to stem the decay, but an effort he believed in with all his heart. An effort he was willing to die for. And as I stood in that dark and ever warming corridor, while my teammates ascended the shaft, I saw that same devotion and dedication to that very same effort in Miranda. An effort she was willing to die for. I had to get out. I had to survive. Or the chances, however slight they seemed, that Morgan and Miranda had given to me would be for naught. I didn't know what I could do with this chance, but I knew I couldn't let it simply slip away. I raced back to the command room and began frantically searching for more knives. Not a soldier within earshot. Miranda had all of their attention. I found one in a drawer, then another, then two more on a rack on a wall. When I had gathered enough, I ran back to my teammates. Stevenson was barely a third of the way up, Jenkins followed, and Givvens stood waiting for my return.

"Here, everyone use two knives and climb up hand-over-hand. Givvens, pass these up to Jenkins and tell him to give one to Stevenson."

Givvens did as I asked and soon we were making double time up the shaft. After nearly 30 minutes of climbing, Stevenson reached the exit and crawled up onto the dry debris-strewn earth. The rest of us followed. We sat where we came up, cringing and panting, drained by the climb. Not a minute had passed when Givvens turned to the south at the sound of clanking metal hitting the ground in rhythmic succession. Then there was rumbling and the earth shook.

"Oh for fuck's sake NOW what!?" Stevenson groaned.

"It's our vaunted reinforcements" I said with a sneer, nodding my head in the direction of a giant mech just emerging from the rubble.

It stood 5 meters tall, clad in dusky grey metal plates. Three-toed feet on powerful reverse-joint legs lead up to a core shaped like an egg, with arms sticking out of either side. Each arm boasted an array of weapons; machine guns, rockets, anti-tank rifles, rapid-fire plasma cannons, grenade launchers, the works. Two more mechs came stomping and crashing through, followed by several APCs and at least a hundred soldiers on foot clad in full body armor and armed to the teeth with energy weapons. It was a force to be reckoned with and could have easily dispatched the Black Hand soldiers that had ambushed us with hardly a casualty. Just as that thought came to fruition, I was reminded of the horrible truth that we had discovered down in that cave. Just behind the Neo United Nations force was an equally sizeable detachment of Black Hand soldiers with tanks and mechs of their own. It seemed the organization that we worked for, that we had trained for so many years to become an elite arm of, and the Black Hand, were one in the same. We had resigned ourselves to capture and torture or worse when we heard gunfire coming from a few dozen meters to the west, near the entrance to the underground base. We heard cries of pain, and saw muzzle flashes coming from the entrance, but before we could react, Miranda came ripping out of the entrance, splattered with blood, her uniform torn to shreds and nearly gone, wielding only her knife and disemboweling a Black Hand soldier, carrying him with her as she moved out into the open. She tossed the body aside, picked up his rifle and fired wildly back into the tunnel. She reached down, took a grenade off the dead soldier's belt and tossed it into the entrance. The explosion toppled the ground above and sprayed dust and debris into her face; she didn't even flinch. She threw the gun down angrily and looked up to see the massive assault force surrounding and corralling us. She sprinted forward. I thought she might try to stop and reason with them. I never could have imagined what came next. Stevenson roared.

"HEY! WHAT EXACTLY THE FUCK IS GOING ON HERE!?"

Barely a second after he finished, a tranquillizer dart, shot from somewhere in the distance unseen, stabbed Stevenson in the neck and he fell limp to the ground. Several more darts hit Jenkins and Givvens but I was spared. I called out to Miranda. She turned to me, veering toward the nearest mech and before it even noticed there was anything near it, she leapt up its leg and onto its back. Raising her knife above her head, she stabbed down vigorously with both hands and plunged the blade into the top of the mech's head with so much force it cracked open and her arms went down into its core. Its arms dropped and its legs gave out from under it, the entire thing crumpling in on itself and falling to the ground with a thunderous crash. The other mechs and many of the soldiers turned their attention to the downed robot and as they approached, one of the arms suddenly loosed its arsenal, almost all at once. Rockets spiraled out and smashed into walls, exploding and sending chunks of metal and stone cascading down on the soldiers. The machine and plasma guns blistered forth and sprayed out over a wide area. I fell to the ground and covered my head, turning it slightly and shifting my arms to try and see what was happening. The grenade launcher flung off several rounds that arced like mortars and came spinning down, exploding just over the ground, blasting soldiers apart and sending solid metal spears flying into the other mechs and APCs. The APCs started emptying, pouring more soldiers onto the battlefield. I sat up a bit and looked for Miranda. She was crouched behind the downed mech, her hands inside its head, apparently giving it override commands to fire, even in its disheveled state. More rockets loosed and the guns continued to pelt their ranks. Miranda zipped around the mech and between streams of gunfire, leapt up onto another mech, and performed the same attack, stabbing straight into the top of its head and brining it down.

I couldn't believe what I was seeing. This couldn't be humanly possible. Then I remembered. I recalled again the day my brother left for the academy and thought of the last thing he said to me before he walked out of his apartment and I never saw him again. "Don't worry about me little bro. There's a special program within spec ops. They say if you survive it, it makes you into the ultimate soldier. That's what I'm gonna be. So no worries alright? It'll take an awful lot to knock your big bro outta the game!" I hadn't understood what he meant. But even seeing the culmination of this special program in person was only one piece of the puzzle.

Miranda was weaving through soldiers, moving so quickly, and with such erratic jolts that the soldiers couldn't keep up. They would fire where she was, or where they thought she was about to be but wasn't, or they would hit their own soldiers, or their own mechs or APCs as she dodged and ducked around them, somehow always just out of their bullet's reach, using their own vehicles for cover. With only her knife she stabbed through chests and ribcages, pierced through metal plating, and sliced off the arms of mechs. She ran straight at an APC and leapt from the ground to its top, pulling the hatch off like a ration's lid and dropping into it, slaughtering the soldiers waiting within and bursting out of its rear door, onto the next. Explosions and blood and screams and debris and then…silence. I stood up and peered through a giant cloud of dust and smoke, looking for signs of life. Miranda emerged from the chaos; gashes, cuts, slashes and scrapes from shrapnel and bullet grazes dotted her body but there wasn't a single serious wound to be seen save for the hole in her shoulder, now half the size it was when it was fresh. Her hair hung messily over her face as she shambled towards me, still clutching her knife. I stared at her in a stupor of shock and chagrin. How? How can this be?

Before Miranda could reach me, a loud high-pitched squeal that seemed to come from everywhere at once pierced the silence. I cringed in pain and covered my ears, but Miranda screamed and fell to the ground, writhing in agony. I moved toward her but as I did, dust from the ground flew into my face in a swirl. I looked up, still covering my ears, to see a large black helicopter descending almost on top of me. I ran out of the way and the chopper landed equally between where I was standing, and where Miranda lay, curled up in the fetal position and grasping her head in pain. The doors of the chopper slid open and out stepped Commander Tritium. I looked into the chopper and saw Wheatly and Christiansen, bloodied and bound, sitting inside with their eyes pressed closed and their heads hung.

I called out to Miranda as the Commander approached and spoke to her in a rhinal, rough, and resounding voice.

"You have done very *very* well young lady. I do believe our little project has been a success. You have exceeded our expectations, that much is certain but…there's one little issue I'd like to resolve."

The Commander raised his hand and in it was a small black remote with a single grey button. He pressed it and instantly the ringing sound ceased, along with Miranda's pain.

"Now, get up!" he commanded. Miranda rose to her feet, her head tilted forward, her hair covering her face.

"It seems from the battlefield reports I've been getting that you may have developed feelings for one of your soldiers. That you may be…caring for him. This is unacceptable. They are pawns to be used at your will, to die in your stead so that you can complete any mission you are given, regardless of the situation. You have proven yourself more than capable of handling even such dire circumstances as these on your own, but this relationship is dangerous at least, and potentially catastrophic to our program at worst. You must eliminate this soldier immediately, like you would any other obstacle to your perfection. Take this pistol and execute that man. Now."

I realized with ease what he meant. I recalled that the only time Miranda had been seriously hurt was when she was paying more attention to me, to us, than to anything else. Miranda grabbed the weapon without looking and began to walk menacingly toward me. Covered in dirt and blood and nearly naked she stood; still and emotionless, a paragon of destruction stripped down and visceral, almost vulnerable in her bare and tattered state, pure and primal. She raised the weapon and pointed it at my face. The Commander yelled from a distance.

"Do it! You are the pinnacle of combative science, the ultimate soldier, the goddess of death! You already have all the potential you need to make a difference! Erase this final obstruction!"

The explosives we had rigged in the underground base detonated, shaking the ground beneath us and collapsing a huge section next to us, dirt and dust pluming into the sky. Tears slipped down my cheeks as I looked at Miranda with nothing but pity. She had been just like Morgan. Just like me. We wanted to make a difference, seek justice, set things right; ignorant of the depths to which humanity had sunk. To satisfy the selfishness of a few, the needs of many had been sacrificed, and this was no different. Miranda was torn away from herself and transformed into what the world wanted her to be. She sought a path of righteousness and truth but found only deceit and manipulation. Her ideals and her beliefs were no longer her own but a product of her choices, her environment, and the will of a planet filled with people that had forgotten what it meant to be truly free.

"I'm sorry Jason", Miranda said to me. And she pulled the trigger. But that was not the end of my story. Like Miranda, the world wanted more from me than I could give, and it had to kill me to get it.

＊＊＊＊＊＊＊＊＊＊＊

I awoke with a quake and a gasp, staring out through thick convex glass down a long grey corridor, lit only by weak pale white fluorescence. My hair was wet and in my face and I couldn't tell where the light was coming from; only that it was enough to illuminate a series of glass tubes just like mine. A strong wave of deja vu splashed into me; I was sure I had been in this exact place before, and had this exact feeling. I tried to move my arms but found them strapped to the interior with a material altogether unfamiliar. It wasn't metal or cloth, but some odd amalgamation of the two. They gave under my strength, but felt as if they would break my wrists should I try to escape them. My legs and feet were fastened the same way. Twice I smacked the back of my head against the padding behind me, the second harder than the first. I clenched and bared my teeth, frantically scanning the room for any sign of life or movement. Without warning, plumes of steam shot out from the sides of several of the other tubes and slowly the glass lifted open, an eerie mist pouring out from them. Suddenly my straps snapped open. Another test. Even after annihilating an entire battalion and a half, they still thought I needed more testing, more training, more killing. It has been a heavy price I've paid to get this far. To give up now would mean every life lost because of my actions was in vain.

I kicked and shattered the door of my glass cage and rolled forward out of it. In nothing but underwear, I found my knife still fastened to a belt around my waist. I drew it to my left hand and waited, my eyes darting back and forth. Something pushed through the mist in the distance and was coming towards me, slicing through it, an ethereal swell not seen or heard but felt. Just before it reached me I sensed a tangible exigency, a very human desire to be over and done with this task. Its urgency gave it away too soon. I titled back, spreading my arms, falling towards the floor but catching myself on my elbows. I heard the unmistakable swish of a blade and felt its wind not an inch from my nose. Sparks flew as it clanged against the side of the tube just to the left of mine. No time to think; I lunged forward with my knife but to my dismay connected with nothing. Just then, another swell approached from my right, much faster this time, and larger. I spun to my left, swinging again with my knife where I imagined the first opponent to be but again I hit nothing. I stared at where it seemed the second form was coming from and though there was nothing to see but parting fog, somehow I envisioned this massive humanoid beast, clad in a skin tight suit, his muscles bulging through, his teeth clenched and bared, like mine, through a black featureless mask, and swinging a 2 meter long sword at my head. But I could tell it wasn't focused. It was thinking only of its attack, very obviously ignoring any danger to itself, like a predator putting it all on the line for what may be its last chance at prey. I felt the pressure of the air of its blade and ducked down underneath its swing, the top of the blade scraping across my hair, shearing off a handful of strands. I tumbled forward and stuck my knife into its gut. I felt the unmistakable gouging of flesh, but also the all too familiar tearing of wires and circuits. I put my empty hand flat against its stomach and with all my strength lifted it up with both hands, tossing it back into the dark corner from which it emerged. I knew I had taken too long. I knew my other opponent had seen my opening, and was moving in. I was counting on it. I turned just slightly to my left and felt the tinge of a very thin, very sharp blade across my left arm, cutting fast and deep. With my right hand I grabbed at where it seemed the blade was as it dragged across my arm and clasped it. A shock of pain went through my palm, up my arm, and into my shoulder, reminding me of my failure in the command center, that I was still just flesh and blood. But there was no time for weakness. I let out a primeval scream of agony and anger and pulled my enemy towards me by his own sword, feeling for its opposite shoulder. I wrapped my arm around its neck, tossed my knife to my right hand with the same motion, and shoved it through the bottom of its jaw so that it popped out the top of its head. It fell to its knees and as it did, at last I got to see who or what I was fighting. Swirls of electric sparks and crackles of light shimmered about him as he fell face first on the ground. It appeared to be merely a man but I knew better. The suit he wore was unlike anything I had seen before. It was mostly black, interspersed with charcoal grey bands that sunk in slightly. Across those bands, shimmers of light continued to flow. The mask was so dark it looked like a hole in the floor. As I observed the body, I realized the shape and size of my defeated foe was no accident. It was nearly a perfect match for me. I wondered why I never saw this before. So much of the past 10 years had been fabricated, designed to put me on a specific path, send me out in such a manner so as to almost guarantee a particular response. Each mission was a test of different skill sets, an examination of my progression, and added experience and prowess. I had followed the bread crumbs this far without even realizing such an obvious path had been laid out before me. They wanted me to run through their maze, and I needed to find out what was at the end of it. I stripped the body as fast as I could, donned the suit and mask, and picked up the blade. Short, balanced, nearly weightless, and razor sharp; made of the same material as my knife. I heard the distinctive echoing smack of metal against metal. All I had to do was think it and the suit tightened, molding around my body as if it were my own skin. A second later, in a dim flash and a quiet shimmer, I was gone. Tens of thousands of tiny fiber optic cameras on every inch of the suit each recorded real time images of whatever was in front of it, and simultaneously projected the image of the camera directly opposite it. I may as well have been a thin pane of glass, difficult to spot even with drastic movements, impossible to detect while still. And still I was, waiting patiently for whatever the hell was coming next.

Two hulking visages pushed through the mist. Clad in full body armor black as a cloud-covered night sky. They had no intention of hiding themselves like my previous foes. They stood almost 3 meters tall, 2 meters across at the shoulders; their eyes glowed a shocking bright orange and swirled slowly. Each had an arm that was no longer their own, but a grotesque compilation of flesh and steel. Each ended in a large tube, bored clockwise and menacing. On each of their shoulders sat a metal box filled with high explosive rockets that they held in place with their other arm. Each step they took sent vibrations through the platform beneath my feet. It quickly became apparent my new suit would not hide me from them completely. Within seconds, the one on the left raised his cannon, and the one on the right knelt down and I heard a loud click as the safety was taken off the rocket launcher. I rushed forward as fast as I could. The left cyborg fired his cannon, the thunk of the shot sounding almost identical to the Mark Six. I stepped heavy onto my right foot mid-stride and the ball of super-heated plasma shot past me, missing my wounded shoulder by a few centimeters. I reached the right cyborg just as the engines of several rockets ignited. I flipped backward and kicked upward at the launcher, causing the rockets to shoot into the ceiling and blast a hole in it, revealing another sub-level to the facility. I knew that whatever sensors they were equipped with could detect me, but I also knew that these behemoths were far too slow to keep up with me. I darted between the two and as I did, the left cyborg took a shot at me with his cannon and hit his comrade straight in the chest. The right cyborg stumbled back, dropping his launcher. I turned and as the smoke cleared I could see almost no damage was done. This would be harder than expected.

I ran down the hallway. The left cyborg switched to his rockets and the right to his cannon and both unloaded at me. Cannon blasts flew past and around me and I could hear the screech of the rockets closing in. I tuned a corner just in time and the payload hit the end of the corridor with such force that I flew forward and landed flat on my face. I sprang up immediately and ran into the hole the blast had left. Right away I noticed a service ladder leading up to a sealed hatch. I replaced my knife in my belt, clenched my sword between my teeth, and climbed. As I neared the door I reached back with my good arm and punched as hard as I could. The hatch flew off its hinges and I rose up to the next level, switching my sword back to my right hand. My cloak still active, I tip-toed back the way I came until I reached the hole the first barrage of rockets had blasted in what was now the floor. Carefully I removed my knife from my belt, aimed for the nearest pipe I could see on the level below, and threw. The pipe burst with a clang and even more steam poured into the corridor, whooshing and hissing. I could hear the thudding footsteps of the clumsy cyborgs coming closer. They had fallen for it. I waited patiently, hardly breathing, every muscle relaxed but ready. The pair passed slowly under the hole before me. I knew it. Weak spot. There was armor where the helmet met the chest plate at the back of the neck but it was primarily textile in composition, probably spider silk. Strong and flexible, but not nearly as dense as whatever the rest of their armor was made of. I straightened up and grasped my sword with both hands, pointing it straight down. I knew I would only get one shot. I jumped through the hole and plunged my blade into the back of the left cyborg's neck. It sunk through and I could feel the soft give of a warm living body. The monster threw his head back and screamed in agony, simultaneously reaching back to grab at me. As it did, its rocket launcher began to fall forward off its shoulder. I yanked my sword out of the cyborg's innards and swiped clean across the back of the launcher, removing the propulsion segment, thereby activating the warheads. I stood up on the cyborg's shoulders and jumped, grabbing onto the edge of the hole and flipping myself over and up, back onto the level above me. The rockets hit the ground tip first and all of them detonated, sending a seething column of searing blue flame up through the hole. I threw myself backwards and out of its way. The entire corridor shook. As the noise of the explosion died down I slowly approached the hole again and cautiously looked through. The cyborg I had stabbed lay flat on his face, motionless, half charred. The other cyborg was nowhere to be seen. I dropped through the hole.

As soon as I hit the floor, a cannon shot came screeching at me, but I ducked under it and it impacted the wall behind me. The afterglow of the cyborg's cannon gave it away and I charged toward it, low as I could get without losing too much speed. I couldn't see it yet but I could sense it; feel its movements, almost before it made them. Launcher gone, it raised its empty fist to smash me as I approached. I slipped just slightly to the side and sliced upwards at its shoulder.

Just as I thought, there was only spider silk covering the under part of its arm and my blade sliced right through it, stopping at the solid shoulder plate. The cyborg roared in pain as its arm fell limp but it wasn't giving up. It aimed its cannon for a point blank shot but my cloak aided me just enough that the projectile missed over my outside shoulder. Its cannon glowed bright red with heat but it quickly tilted the imposing arm towards me for another shot. I slipped my sword blade-first into the barrel and as the ball of plasma formed and tried to escape, most of it backfired into the arm, blowing it clean off, the remainder of the blast splashing harmlessly against my suit. The cyborg stumbled back, barely able to express the excruciating pain it must have been feeling, but still it would not give in. The cyborg tore at me head first, attempting to pin me up against the nearest wall. It was able to catch me and push me a couple of meters but it didn't last; I slid down and kicked its feet out from under it. It tripped and fell face first onto the ground. Immediately it began to try and right itself with the stump of its cannon arm, and push up with the other. It rose to one knee and grabbed something off the floor I could not at first make out. It raised it over its head and began to bring it down and I realized what was happening. It was a rocket warhead that had not detonated, somehow knocked away from the explosion and left active, but intact. With almost no time to think I looked down and kicked the first random piece of metal scrap that I saw. Just as the tip of the rocket was about to hit the floor, the scrap metal connected with the cyborg's hand, knocking the rocket out of it and sending it tumbling into the mist. The cyborg turned to chase after its only chance but before it could move towards it I was on top of its back. I stuck down with both my fists at the back of its neck. The cyborg convulsed and collapsed but not before it had spun around much faster than I thought it could and flung me off of its back and onto mine. It groaned and grunted, propped itself into a sitting position and just sat there, breathing slow and deep with a cold metallic heave. Torn circuits and wires were exposed and crackling and he was leaking magnetorheological fluid. Robot blood, but much thicker and darker than anything I had ever seen from any mech. I stood and stared. Something wasn't right. This one had fought so hard. It had been smart enough not to shoot at me as I passed between the two of them, though its comrade was not. It was able to survive the explosion, and fought me nearly limbless. I approached the fallen beast slowly. I stood before it, a handful of centimeters from its face and I knew it could see me. I pulled off my mask and as I did, my suit shimmered and crackled and my cloak deactivated. The cyborg heaved louder and faster. Its eyes, now dimmed and pulsing, seemed to widen and tremble. I was so stunned by this reaction that I just stood there, staring in surprise for a moment. I collected myself and turned to retrieve my knife. I found it stuck into the wall behind the pipe I had burst with it, yanked it out, and returned to my disabled foe. I thought it best to end its suffering. However much physical pain it was in, I was certain it could not match the realization of the loss of its soul. I raised my knife to strike, but its eyes turned unmistakably from shock to fear. I knew how dangerous it was, what I was thinking of doing. What if it catches me off guard? What if what I find destroys my perception, my ability to function as a soldier? All the years I'd spent playing their game blind, only to see it for what it truly was now would be wasted. I recalled that day on my parents farm, when I was a girl who knew nothing of the dark places of the world, the desolate corners of the human heart. All the time between the few days after I left for the academy and now seemed a lifeless blur, an aimless string of training and battles and violence. Yet all this time I had kept a tiny piece of myself closed off from all of it; a serenitous sanctuary to lay my humanity down in while I trekked through wastelands and the barren minds of the people who presided over them. I had put it to sleep inside myself so that one day, when the time was right, I could awaken it, combine it with all my newfound strength and force the change I wanted so desperately to enact. I was in danger of losing it forever. Of become nothing more than the indurate instrument of death and destruction the world wanted me to be. I would not have it. I turned my knife and in a flash sliced through the spider-silk armor covering the cyborg's neck just enough to cut it open without cutting its flesh. I stuck my knife in my belt, leaned forward, grasped the bottom of the helmet and pulled it off. Immediately I inhaled in horror; my eyes burned and my voice trembled.

"Jason! No. No, it can't be true, how…how could they have done this to you I…oh god I'm sorry. I'm so very sorry…I didn't think they would, I mean, when I shot you I…oh no…no no NO!"

His face was pale green, covered in blue and purple veins. His eyes glowed that same burning orange but were unfocussed and faint. He was gasping for air. I saw the hole in his cheek I had given him. Quickly I replaced his helmet and his breathing steadied. My aim at that range, with that much time to concentrate, was impeccable. The bullet went through his cheek, about an inch to the right of the bottom of his nose, at such an angle that it would only barely graze the edge of the medulla, and the bottom of the cerebellum. This would instantly knock him unconscious and reduce his brain, heart, and respiratory functions to the bare minimum, nearly undetectable by anything but the most sensitive of instrumentation. A lesser man would be dead in hours, perhaps minutes, but not Jason. Of all the soldiers I had served with, fought alongside and watched die over the years, Jason was different. His strength came not from his intellect or his muscle, though he both in abundance. It came from the same place mine came from. An ethereal center, fixated and unwavering, oblivious to opinion or judgment, comprehending the fundamental and unarguable difference between the unequivocal right, and the clear conspicuous wrong. He would not give up. He would not let go. They would think he was dead, they would let him alone, perhaps even leave him where he lay, and in a day or two he would heal enough to regain consciousness and move. He would drag himself to safety, however he could. Such was my timid hope. The only one I could see for him in that moment, lest we both be destroyed.

I had seen cyborg prototypes before. Fallen soldiers retained some brain activity for a few hours after death so long as the brain itself was mostly undamaged. If they were retrieved and artificially supported with basic functions, scientists and engineers could then graft electrical and mechanical instruments and weapons onto them, stuff whatever was left of their organs with microchips. They retained their more recent memories, their combat experience, instincts, everything you would want from a good solider. But they had no emotional connection to any of it. Their brains were more akin to organic super computers, possessed of a human being's uncanny ability to adapt and adjust, but without any persuasions getting in the way of pure battlefield logic. Perhaps they really did think Jason was dead. And even though they detected brain damage they decided to use him anyway. Did they find out he was alive during the process and go ahead with it? Did they kill him for sure and then turn him into this thing? Just as all of this was ricocheting around in my mind Jason spoke, his voice hollow and distant.

"I'm sorry Miranda. I didn't know it was you. I would have helped you if I had known. But then, I guess you didn't need my help."

"Jason, oh god, how did this happen? What's the last thing you remember?"

"I remember everything. I realized when the back of my head hit the ground and it hurt that I wasn't dead. I...ughhhh ahhhhhh!"

"I'm sorry, never mind, don't talk any more, here let me...I can take parts from the other cyborg and try to...repair you. Christ, repair you, this is all my fault, I wasn't strong enough, I'm fucking never gonna be strong enough!"

"Miranda...we're both still here. We can still do something. You haven't come this far to give up now, and neither have I."

As I looked at his disheveled form I felt myself nearly burst into tears at my failure to protect him. I half choked, then almost laughed aloud. Even after he had been grafted into a machine, his body no longer his own, he still had a firm grip on his hope. It filled me with a singular happiness pure as the placid pond of my childhood. He didn't leave me alone. He stayed. Through all the torment and back from the precipice of death, he stayed. His strength was greater than mine. Then it hit me. This was the difference. Jason was the difference. Always alone had I persevered against the subliminal suggestions, the brutal conditioning, the genetic and molecular tampering, battle after battle after battle trying to break down my will and rebuild in its place only the desire to kill. I had never had someone to count on, someone to help me. Someone who could tip the scales, turn the tide, and from the inside no less. The Commander and his team had designed this test so that we would never know who we were fighting until it was too late. And it nearly was. They didn't count on Jason. But I did. I walked over to and grabbed the other fallen cyborg by the arms and slowly dragged his body over to where Jason sat. He squinted at the from and slowly his face melted into sorrow.

"They didn't just take me Miranda. They took everyone."

I flipped the body over, pulled the helmet off, and fell to my knees.

"Jenkins. Oh...I'm sorry Marc. I did this to you. I wasn't strong enough to save you. Only to end you. Please forgive me. I will...I will avenge you."

"There was nothing you could have done. It wasn't time yet. I know, I understand..."

His voice faltered but he shook off the pain and the fear and spoke to me again, stronger than before.

"If you had tried to fight them, all the Commander would have to do is push that button. All of us, we are sacrifices to a worthy cause. Just not the one we thought. Jenkins would have been glad to give his life for you. We all would. Without even knowing what we were really fighting, what you were really up against. We felt it from you. But no one more than me."

I gave Jason a weak, almost pitiful smile then turned my eyes away. I glanced over towards the far end of the corridor where I had slain the two cyborgs with cloaking suits. I had hope still. A fool's hope. I checked the bodies, examined them closely. The smaller one I had stripped of its suit was Wheatley. The larger was Christiansen. They must have been so far gone they didn't even recognize me. That left Stevenson and Givvens. Before I could speak, Jason read my thoughts.

"It figures they would leave Givvens and Stevenson for some other more advanced project. So strong the two of them. Christ who are these people!? Fucking not even people, maniacal vultures more like. Remorseless. How could they…do this to…ughhh their fellow man, their own soldiers…ahhhhh! What is going on here!?"

"Please just, don't talk anymore. Let me work on you."

I gathered all the bodies up near Jason. I knew I had some time. It was a grueling battle after all; I would need time to rest. They always underestimated me. All they had to track me was the tiny device they had implanted somewhere in my head. The same device every spec ops team leader was given in order to 'increase battlefield awareness'. The same device that would send high frequency shock waves and damaging electrical impulses through my body whenever the Commander pushed the button on that remote. Held long enough, it would quite literally vibrate my organs to dust and melt my brain to slush while I lay there helpless. It seemed an insurmountable failsafe. But I would have to worry about that when the time came to get past it, or die.

I thought there was no way they could have seen this coming; that they had no idea what I could put together with just a few rudimentary tools. I searched the corridor high and low. I found an electro-torque wrench, a fusion welder, and some plexi-steel tubing in a maintenance locker. Along with my knife, this was more than I needed. I severed and sliced, dismembered and spliced, fused and fixed and tore and tweaked and worked until I could barely feel my hands. It must have taken me half a day at least. But I didn't just fix Jason. I made him one of the most formidable forces of destruction alive. A fusion of the greatest strengths of all their horrid creations, molded to monstrous perfection. I heated his incredibly dense body armor for hours until it was malleable. I then merged it with Christiansen's cloaking suit, welding it beneath the network of cameras. I took the still-intact cannon arm off Jenkin's cyborg body and attached it to Jason's stump. I gathered up pieces of scrap from his destroyed cannon, and from the rocket launchers and even the steel of the corridor itself and grafted a 2 meter long serrated blade underneath his new arm. I took parts from Wheatley's body and repaired and reinforced the steel and tissue of Jason's free-hand arm, increasing its overall musculature and impact potential. I shaved off armor from his legs to increase his mobility and reprogrammed the software in his helmet that connected to the microchips in his brain to increase his sensor's capabilities, and his power core's potency. Jason went from strong-hearted but subaltern soldier, to potent but ponderous cyborg, to apotheosis of aggression; a harbinger of the hatred he held for the weakness of those we had trusted with our future. He and I together would find a way to the top of this pyramid of presumption, built in a pietistic pit of murder and broken promises, surrounded by a river of lies, or we would die trying. All my life I had waited for my chance. And here it was, within my reach.

Part V

Softly and slowly we walked, conscious of every sound, our eyes snapping to even the slightest hint of light or movement though it always turned out to be just a flashing console or a set of heat exchangers firing, their pistons set into the walls, randomly shifting up and down. I couldn't tell if this was a research facility, a giant test tube, a twisted arena, or some combination. Every corridor was an identical crisscross of dark grey steel, pipes, and cables. We ascended its levels like a staircase, traveling the length of one corridor to find the hatch leading up to the next, only to be placed at the opposite end of the next level's hatch. I had a feeling all of this had been constructed to disguise what was happening in the bowels of this place. I began to wonder if the Neo UN at large knew of the existence of this project, or if it was somehow a well-kept secret. Was the entire military involved in this cabal, or was it only Commander Tritium and his soldiers? And what of the Black Hand? Were they entirely a fabrication? Or was the deception much deeper? Had I been part of the Black Hand the entire time, their officers having created an elaborate ruse, meticulously conceived and cleverly executed, to make me think I had joined the NUN but was theirs all along? Perhaps they intercepted me on route to one of my training facilities, years ago. Limpidity pelted my psyche. The NUN was desperate for soldiers; they were losing the war. Considering that, it would make sense for the Black Hand to have commandeered a sizeable amount of NUN equipment and technology over the years, to have spies planted throughout NUN ranks. It may have been disturbingly easy to kidnap me without me even realizing, naive as I was when I first joined, and use their stolen assets to create the illusion of a NUN base, or even an airship. The Black Hand's forces speckled the land and the NUN was stretched thin, not adequately trained or equipped to deal with the kind of dirty tactics and apparent disregard for life the Black Hand seemed so comfortable with. Who knows what they were capable of with no one to challenge a particular sect for a thousand kilometers in every direction? Or was the war with the Black Hand merely a front to cover the Neo UN's true objectives. No matter how I thought about it, one thing was clear; we were all of us deceived, honorable soldiers blinded by our own barely controllable desire to make a difference…to matter. Special Forces. The best of the best. Now we are dead, or worse; lusus naturae, subservient to vicious and cruel overlords who seek to wield us as insensible weapons against their hated enemy, for reasons beyond our empathy or understanding. But at least we still had each other. Somehow, Jason was still by my side.

Finally we reached a hatch that looked different from the rest. It was bright red with white stripes and the words "Ground Level" were written across the center. Jason and I looked at each other and nodded. I went to climb the ladder but Jason put his oversized hand on my shoulder; the same one that had been wounded what now seemed like ages ago.

"I don't have ultra-dense body armor for nothing. I'll go first"

I moved out of his way. In two steps he was at the hatch and true to his instincts, instead of punching this door off its hinges like we had all the others, he tried pushing it first. It gave only slightly and would likely have flown off its hinges anyway had he pushed with all his might. He looked down at me, as if doing so was helping him think. He turned back to the hatch and suddenly shoved his massive arm-blade through where he guessed the latch on the other side might be, making only a slight scraping sound that didn't seem to echo. He retraced his blade and slowly pushed the hatch open. Without a glance he gave me a thumbs-up, activated his cloak, and passed through. I heard his footsteps towards my left as he walked over me. I cloaked and followed, making sure to rise through the hatch facing the right. The dark grey basementy corridors were replaced by much larger and brighter ones; walls of sectional slates of steel with sheen like aluminum, smooth and symmetrical, winding off into the distance in both directions. Jason turned to me and uttered about the last thing I was expecting.

"Eeny meeny miney moe?"

"Catch a tiger by the are you fucking kidding me…Jason this is not the time for…"

"It's the perfect time. You wanna do it, or should I?"

"I…you…yeah alright, I'll do it. I'm not doing it out loud though. I'm gonna do it in…in my head, okay?"

"You're no fun."

"Holy shit, fine FINE! Ughhhh. Okay…eeny meeny miney moe, catch a tiger by the toe, if he hollers let him go, eeny meeny miney moe."

"Ha! Left it is then. Good choice. Right is always wrong, right?"

"Right…I mean no! Oh whatever, can we go please?"

"Yeah alright hahaha I'm going! Just stay right behind me. That'll hide you from direct line-of-sight sensors too."

"Okay. Lead the way."

How inappropriate of us, yet it was just like before. We went somewhere so far outside what was happening to us that we forgot what was happening to us. A momentary but much needed reprieve. I did as Jason asked and followed closely behind him, covering his footprints. We hadn't the slightest idea what to expect. We followed the corridor's curves for what seemed like hours; we were moving so slowly we probably hadn't gone very far. We were both so very anxious. Our chance to change our fate teetered on the edge of an abyss. The lightest misstep would send us plunging forever into darkness. We would take no chances. We stopped at and checked down every cross-section, our heads making slow circles looking for cameras, trip wires, infrared alarm systems, anything that could give us away. Security was suspiciously light, but we sidestepped a few measures along the way. We arrived at a massive steel door with an open frame displaying a multitude of serious looking locking mechanisms and a pressure seal system designed to keep us in and others out. Jason scanned the door with his sensors, then deactivated his cloak.

"I don't know if I can blast through this. I think it will just lock the door more if you know what I mean."

"The heat from the plasma will just fuse all that stuff together, right. Even if you could it'd make far too much noise. We need to make them open it for us."

"How do we do that?"

My cloak shimmered away as I closed my left hand and put it up to my mouth, grabbing my left elbow with my right hand. I huffed and hunched over, my eyes shifting back and forth, looking inward, searching. Then I started thinking out loud.

"Okay, well…if we blast the door open, assuming we could, the whole place would probably come down on us. But…if we cause a commotion in here…they might just think my battle with their creations spilled out onto this level and send a small team, perhaps just a clean-up crew, while the Commander watches. He has to be relatively close to me for the signal from that…device to hurt me enough to stop me."

"Do you have any idea what that is or how it works?"

"Well I know the signal is on a wavelength that causes physical harm. I can feel what it's doing to me while it's on as if the Commander himself were in my brain trying to squash it. As far as how it achieves that...no idea."

"Do you think it could affect me too now?"

"I can't say for sure. You have a handful of microchips in your brain connected to your suit and to the sensors in your helmet. I'm no cyborg as far as I can tell but I may very well have similar chips. Hey…hey, could you scan me? I mean, use your sensory equipment to locate irregular electrical impulses and try and pinpoint the source. I may be able to do some sort of half-assed surgery on myself to remove the one that receives that signal."

"Well, I'll scan you, but the second part of your plan doesn't sound so good. You could kill yourself trying to take it out. Or more likely taking it out would kill you. But anyway, turn around let me have a look."

I turned and Jason leaned down and over me, his eyes perhaps half a meter from the back of my head. I heard a high pitched whirring and could see an intensified glow out of the corner of my eye. In a few seconds he was done.

"Yeah you've got chips alright. About 15 of them, all in different parts of your brain. Some seem to be connected to your motor control and reflexes, others to your endorphin and adrenaline production, others to your sight, hearing, smell. There's even a couple in your sensory cortext, probably what allows you to shrug off pain so easily. How they hell they got in there without causing any damage I can't imagine. They have tech the like I've never seen before. But I can't tell which one carries the signal for that device the Commander has. Could be all of them. Or maybe it's something else entirely. I'm sorry, I'm no help really. I wonder if you'd be better off without me…"

"Jason don't you ever…EVER talk like that again you understand me!? I would have died if it wasn't for you. My heart, my mind would have died. You made me strong where it really mattered. No amount of enemies I've faced could defeat me, none of their strengths could match mine but I was so close to losing myself, not being able to see my way past the slaughter, but YOU, you pulled me back from the brink of a slow quiet madness because you cared. Because you saw past and into me and through me. And you never gave up on me. So I'll never give up on you. We're in this together. Whatever may come."

I had no idea what expression Jason had. It didn't matter. I knew he heard me.

"Alright so forget about the chips for now, how about you test out the modifications I made to your plasma cannon and start blasting random holes in the walls?"

"Yes ma'am, I mean, Lieutenant!"

Jason aimed down a corridor leading off to the right of the sealed door, charged up a powerful shot, and fired. The basketball sized bright blue and green glowing ball of superheated energy screamed down the dark hallway into blackness. A few seconds later we heard a deep rumble and the walls near us vibrated.

"You missed."

"What!? I didn't know that corridor was like 200 meters long, it's pitch dark 20 meters in, my seneors aren't THAT good!"

"Haha alright, okay! Damn…"

"I'm sorry I…why did I get so angry? I've never snapped at you like that before."

"Hey, don't worry about it."

"No wait a second, I can't scan myself, what if the chips I have in my head are doing something to me?"

"It's possible I suppose. But once we get close to him you can hang back and use your cannon. I'll do what I have to do to get close enough to throw my knife into whichever of his hands is holding the remote. Then it's all over."

"Yeah, but what if it can also control us? What if the strength they see in you is your ability to receive the upgrades these chips provide without having to meld you with metal?"

"I don't understand…what…"

"All this power you have isn't just from a bunch of chips, you know that. There's a reason we've seen 4 cyborgs so far including me, and there's only 1 you. You're clearly superior to us…I mean look at the hunk of junk I was stuck in! Maybe the signal will just gigantically amplify my anger, connected to whatever chip changed my mood so easily like that, and send me wailing at the first thing I see."

"That's ridiculous, you're just be-"

"Is it though!? Look at where we are! Look at what's happened to us! They can't duplicate you. They can't control you. But you're probably the most deadly armed force on this planet right now and you're only getting stronger, more resourceful, less remorseful. They can't mind control you, so they're gonna brainwash you, everything that's happened so far is to push you towards that end. They're gonna throw obstacle after obstacle at you until you meet one you would never have dared remove…but you do."

"What kind of obstacle could that possibly be?"

"Me. And you upgraded the fuck out of me so if you had to fight me you'd have to be serious, you'd have to really come after me. And you did it yourself. FUCK I should have seen this coming!"

"Well, okay wait let's…think about this for a minute…"

No sooner than a handful of seconds into that minute and the pressure door before us clicked loudly, and the pistons and the lock's centerpiece began to shift and turn. Thick steam, fog in form and visual texture, weaseled its way in from the edges and corners of the doorframe, like smoke from a backdraft. Jason turned and pierced me with the vex of his stare, furious and terrified. I knew what I had to do. Slowly the door peeled open, scrapping against its frame, the gap now 10 centimeters…30…50…1 meter and I dashed forward with just enough space for me to run through shoulder to shoulder, but not nearly enough for Jason's much larger body.

"Miranda WAIT!"

I was gone into shadow.

****

I reached out my hand as if I could have somehow snatched her back from that engulfing swarth. I was not as slow as I had been but there was no chance, no possible way I could catch up to her. They wanted me to follow her. Without seeing her. And we would fall into their trap. They would lead us into a tiny room together with impenetrable walls, a low ceiling, nothing in it, and no way out. And only one of us would survive. If it was her then what humanity is left in her will be gone and she will give up and belong to them. If it was me…then I just killed the last hope we had of stopping them. But if I don't go, she may never even make it to the Commander, or to the trap, and I may never know. Never know if I could have helped, if I should have. If I would have been the difference. How could I go? How could I stay? My only choice? I back up and watch as the door slowly finishes swinging past me, take a deep breath, and step through. I had to find her first. If I could get to her before whatever trap they laid had sprung, then the last thing they were expecting would happen. The Commander will be close to watch his two masterpieces, one created by the other; he won't be able to help himself. We will spring on him. We will catch him off guard, and we will end this. No more than five steps in and I heard the door slam behind me. I didn't even turn to look at it. What little light there was in this new and foreboding corridor was gone. With my infrared sensors, I could see a few meters in front of me in a small cone, so I slowly panned around as I walked, trying to cover as much of my environment as I could. The corridor grew wider the farther in I went, slowly expanding up and out, shaping into a planate pentagon large enough to fly a small jet fighter through. An abrupt and eerie series of distant clinks drew my attention as far down the corridor as I could manage to see. The clinks multiplied until it sounded like rain against a drainpipe. Several heavy grates flipped open and a stream of spider-like robots poured out from them. Their legs formed near perfect arches as they rolled around in ball joints propelling the creations forward at a tenacious pace. Their bodies were translucent trapezohedrons with dim undulations of light coming from the cores. I knew by the sound that were flooding the passageway, and that the only way past them was through them. I shut down my cloaking system so that I could relay all the energy I could spare to my arms. As the first several spiders neared, their cores began to glow and a point of light focused itself at the head of their bodies, firing brilliant white beams that lit up the corridor like the moon would an otherwise shadowy night. I swayed from left to right to left, my arms up in front of my face like a shield. Some of the blasts missed me, some smacked into my forearms and I felt a kind of drilling pressure, like the shots were less trying to stab through me as they were trying to bore into me. But my armor held. I quickened my pace, trying to build enough moment to knock the spiders over as I ran past them, my feet thudding with each step, faster and faster, as more and more spiders filled the chamber. With my arms still in front of my face I could only glance around them to see where I was going. My feet found the incline before my eyes but it wasn't as though I hobbled into the incline; it came up to meet me. The room was shifting. They were trying to push me back, force me into a deadening duel with these things, one I would likely win but would take a lot of time.

I stopped and looked down, using my new sensory enhancements to see through the floor and down to the next level. Directly below me was an imposing mechanism; a large rectangular block with rounded edges rose up into an arm about half the size of the block itself. The arm seemed to extend up to somewhere a few meters behind me. I turned, but as I did, 6 spiders where within a meter of me; 2 had moved around almost behind me. They crouched and leapt at me, each one aiming for a different part of my body, all connecting at once; one on each of my legs, each of my arms, my chest, and the back of my head. Almost instantly they all started to glow. Kamikaze. The Divine Wind. A sea of self-destructing robots, marching relentlessly. This was a small piece of the force they were creating. Cyborgs, superhumans, uncountable waves of these things…and Miranda was their army's centerpiece, a dark and beautiful jewel ornamenting the top of a dozer blade meant to shove the world over the threshold and send it toppling into a millennia of savagery and despair.

The light from the suicide spiders illuminated almost the entire passageway and just before me I caught the shadow of what looked to be the plate attached to the arm, slowly pushing half the room up. I turned down the intensity of my cannon, leaned back, aimed and fired at its center, simultaneously punching a hole in the rising floor behind me, then slipping my hand through and gripping tight. My shot connected, piercing the attached plate without breaking the arm away. This caused what I guessed was the pressure control system to malfunction and sent the floor of half the room shooting up at incredible speed. All the spiders attached to me when flying off, and all around me spiders fell, bouncing off each other and tumbling to the lower half of the room, falling on top of the spiders that had been coming from behind me. I was in the lower part of the floor-wall, so I turned to climb but realized I only had one hand. I looked at my blade and noticed a swivel mechanism just where the base of it met my elbow. Miranda thought of everything. She wanted to take care of me. I sent a mental command through my suit and my blade dropped into a perpendicular position and locked into place. I alternated stabbing my blade through the wall, and pounding another hole into the cheap steel, creating handhold after handhold. After a few seconds of climbing, I looked down to see the spiders regrouping and climbing on top of each other to create a moving path up to me. I fired off a couple of quick shots but they glanced off their reflective armor coating. These things liked to get close and were meant to be taken down close. While firing, my sensors analyzed my foe, trying to ascertain any weak points. Miranda would have already known them by now. In fact she probably knew how to sneak past them undetected, which is why they only showed up when I did. Stealth mode was not one of my stronger modes. I learned that their explosive cores were triggered by a voluntary internal overheat, but that unless their cores reach a certain temperature, they won't detonate, only crumble. That must have been what happened to the ones that fell off me. So most long range weapons and certainly any traditional solid round ammunition would set them off, but stepping on them wouldn't. I knew I had to get up to the top and find a way out. I was sure the spiders would be close behind, but they would be staggered in groups, not an open sphere closing in all around me. All the better for me to squash them.

I reached the edge of the vertical floor, pulled myself up and stood atop it. Looking down I saw the self-made ladder of spiders was not far off. Looking up I realized I was still a good 3 meters away from the ceiling. The first thing I did was redirect as much energy as I could to my cannon and shot a huge blast clean through the ceiling. What I needed to do was risky to say the least, but it was the only way out. I looked back down below me and tried to find the spider that was closest to reaching me. Just before it could pull itself up to the edge where I was, I reached down and grabbed it, holding it up in front of my face. Sure enough it began to glow. I had no idea how long exactly it would take for this thing to blow. I just had to judge it, pay close attention to the intensity and sense it. Another few seconds later there were several more spiders nearly up to the edge. With nothing left but luck that my timing was right, I jumped straight up into the air as high as I could manage and at once threw the spider I was holding at the spiders that were just coming up onto the ledge. Just as I reached the apex of my leap, the spider I had thrown exploded just above his counterparts causing a chain reaction that destroyed several dozen nearby spiders, creating a massive balloon-like explosion. I shielded my face with my arms and was launched high into the air, right through the hole I had made. As I passed through, I pointed my cannon arm straight out and, still at near maximum power, fired in front of me. I wasn't aiming for anything. I needed the recoil. I barely felt it with my feet firmly planted on solid ground, but suspended in mid-air it became a rocket boost that propelled me backwards and away from the hole. I rolled over myself a couple time before ending up in a sitting position just a couple of meters away from my impromptu escape hatch. I could still hear the permeating chatter of the spiders scrambling to find a way up to me but I was safe for the moment. I picked myself up and rotated slowly in place to get some bearing on my new surroundings. Much like the transition from the depths of this place to wherever I had just been, the contrast was salient. Instead of large, long, mostly empty, and decidedly uninviting corridors of hot steam and cold steel, I was surrounded by consoles and monitors, control stations and inactive surgical machines; operating chairs encased in plexiglass, and gigantic computer banks, all lit by fluorescence from the ceiling and behind the wall panels. Rows upon rows of servers lined both sides of the room, buzzing and whirring in their computations, copying and transferring data to and from who knows where. There was a multitude of portable terminals, all with various handheld tools and devices. It all looked to have been abandoned not long ago as much of the equipment was still active, though now seemingly without purpose. I thought about the abominations that must have been thought up and pieced together in this very room. Perhaps I was one of them.

Suddenly, an access vent burst open and 6 spiders crawled out and made their way towards me. I picked up the nearest terminal I saw, lifted it up over my head and flung it at the nearest one, crushing it. I then took two steps forward and kicked another terminal at the next spider, plastering it up against a wall of servers. The 4 remaining spiders were nearly on me, so I held my ground. The first one jumped clumsily at my face and I punched it dead in the center of its body. It broke apart harmlessly. The other 3 jumped together, but I was now just fast enough that I was able to duck out of the way of all but one, who latched onto my right shoulder. It was an impossible angle for me to reach it with my free hand so I quickly turned down my cannon to near minimum intensity and fired a point blank shot at the spider. The shot bounced off its reflective coating like before, but the impact was enough to knock the spider off me and into a control console some 5 meters away. I took two big steps, ending the second with my foot upon one of the two spiders that had missed me and smushed it to dust. The other spun around and jumped at me, but I caught it mid-air. As soon as it started glowing I threw it at the spider I had shot off myself. It contacted its partner and exploded, destroying them both. Pretty good, I thought to myself. But that was just 6 of them. A nearly endless assault, wave after wave of tens of thousands, maybe millions of these things would wear down anyone or anything.
Time to find the way forward. But not before I did away with this room. Chances are our enemies would not lose any valuable data or research, all of it likely backed up in other server banks just like this one, but I'm sure the world would

be better off if I took care of it anyway. Maybe it would at least slow them down, delay their ability to produce their next creation. Besides, it would be fun, if nothing else, and with Miranda gone I had lost so much of my willpower. I needed to feel like there was still a reason to keep going. Maybe destroying this room would help. I set my cannon to moderate intensity and began tossing off shots every which way, blowing apart the servers and terminals, disintegrating monitors and HDDs; after 5 minutes the place was a pile of parts littered with smoldering mounds of plastic, plexiglass and metal. I began searching the edges of the room for an exit. At a far back darkened corner I found a door similar to the one Miranda had disappeared into, but smaller and much thinner. I took several steps back and charged, my shoulder dropped and lined up with the center of the door. At first when I hit I felt almost no give but as my weight and momentum came to bear the door buckled and bent in, pulling out of its own hinges. I threw the door off and stepped in.

Complete darkness lay before me, my sensors picked up nothing. Then all at once light, from what seemed like everywhere. It whited out my vision and my sensors froze. I put my hand up and out in front of me and spread my fingers, trying to block some of the blinding glare. I felt the room shift slightly up and forward, then it felt as if the entire floor had jerked slightly and locked itself in place. Suddenly the room flipped upside down. I free-fell 10 meters and landed flat on my chest. Luckily my armor was strong enough to absorb a good deal of the impact but my cloaking element shimmered across my body until it fizzled and faded. There would be no possibility of retreat for me now. I rose to one knee and then to my feet and looked up at where I had just been standing. The glare gave way to batteries of floodlights and the sound of automatic high powered plasma cannons and straight-shot laser guided strike missiles. Some of the biggest ordinance this side of the pacific, the style of equipment you see on airships and key city-guard bases. My eyes refocused and my sensors rebooted. The room seemed to be rectangular, about 50 meters long and 25 wide. Bigger than I was expecting, but then something happened that hadn't entered my most severe paranoia. Shutters opened in the far wall, revealing 4 sets of slats with windows. With what must have been 100 thousand watts of speaker power, a familiar voice boomed through the arena.

"Jason! Look how far you've come! Do you really think there was any chance you would have made it here if you were nothing but weak flesh and cowardice!?"

"I may have weak flesh but I've NEVER been a coward!"

"Because you've never run from a fight? How very little you know."

The lights dimmed slightly. I could see the openings where all that hardware was pointing at me from. They were everywhere. A sound like a giant vacuum followed by a shudder and a stomp resonated off the walls. A door opened just below the windowed slats. From what could only be described as a giant furnace, Miranda emerged, the glare of murder in her eyes more brilliant than any light. From her back she drew a sword, at least twice as long as the one she had fought me with before, broader and teethed at the base like her knife. She pointed the tip back and down, behind her body like a serpent's tail. She flipped her mask over her face, but instead of a plain skin tight black fabric, the mask was of molded metal in roughly the form of her face, but with flat cheeks and a gaping mouth. She crouched, rushed forward and engaged her cloak, vanishing before my eyes. I had to do something now. I turned my cannon's intensity down to its minimum and began firing off quick bursts of plasma so weak they were barely able to stabilize and detonated in mid-air after only a few meters. As they exploded, pockets of cold blue-white mist formed and hung there. As they warmed to room temperature, the mist became waves of thousands of electric gold and silver spears, blanketing the room. I looked carefully and noticed an arc, just for a moment, where the shower of sparks splashed onto Miranda. I maximized my cannon's energy output and fired at where I thought Miranda was about to be. The shot smacked into the wall in a giant imploding sphere and I saw the distinctive shimmer of cloak when it's trying to adjust to a sudden and significant change in your immediate environment. I charged blade first at her but 5 meters away from me the shimmer stopped and I lost her. I fired a medium intensity shot right where she had disappeared and again the shockwave caused Miranda's suit to shimmer. She was a meter to my left, readying a swipe aimed at my cannon arm's shoulder. I swiveled in her direction just in time and I felt enormous herculean force, as if a car were dropped on my chest; a loud clang echoed and sparks flew. Using the backwards momentum the deflection of her blade gave her, Miranda spun around and lunged straight out and up with her sword, aiming at my neck. I leaned back slightly and countered her blade off to the side. Even before my parry connected, Miranda reached to her belt with her free hand. I gathered myself just in time to put my arm up in front of my face; the knife struck, stabbing clean through and coming out the other side of my arm not 10 centimeters from my nose. I didn't even have time to feel the pain; Miranda stuck her blade in the ground, reached up with her right leg and placed her foot atop the hilt. Like a rocket in strength and an eagle in grace, she launched herself into the air and came down feet first on my collar bone following through with a savage left cross that twisted my neck all the way to one side. I tried to grab her left leg with my right hand but she jumped straight up and out of reach. She summersaulted forward attempting to land behind me. I turned around just in time to catch her foot with my ribcage. I went parallel to the ground, face down, and flew back some 5 meters, landing on my knees and elbows. I tried to stand as quickly as I could but by the time I was rising form my knee, Miranda was face to face with me. She had moved so fast I could have sworn time had slowed down, only for her. She shoved both her hands, palms out, fingers spread, into my stomach. It felt less like I was struck, and more like someone had fastened a massive steel chain to my back, attached it to a jet, and then the jet took off. I folded forwards and went flying backward, my arms and legs straight out in front of me, flailing like a puppet flung across a room. My back smacked into the wall and I slumped down to the floor, grunting and groaning, barely holding onto a conscious state. Then and only then did it really hit me.

She had been holding back the entire time. There had been no murderous spirit before, only the will to survive. This was completely different. She was using all her strength, picking all the right attacks, and pouring the full force of her heart into destroying me. I had no chance. But how could this be what they wanted? I wasn't even a threat to her, never mind a challenge. Miranda walked toward me, her cloak still shimmering from the sparks flying about. I heard her sheath her sword as if to say 'I don't even need this' and she knelt down in front of me, decloaking with her disturbing mask just centimeters from my face. I was sure this was the end; for real this time. But just then, the same door Miranda had emerged from opened again and through my fuzzy malfunctioning sensors I could see what looked to be a dozen or more cyborgs. They marched forward in formation and Miranda turned her attention to them, poised and silent. As they neared and I could observe more detail, I gradually went from baffled, to dismayed, to horrified when I realized that they were near exact copies of me. Clad in anatomically sculpted black armor that hugged their bodies, a cannon with a blade underneath on their left arm, and a free hand on the right. All of them engaged their cloak in unison and vanished. For the first time in I couldn't remember how long, Miranda was visibly shaken. She lowered her stance, stretched out her arms, and began swiveling her head back and forth. I tried to straighten myself up against the wall behind me, still sitting, watching her closely. She turned her back to me, hands still outstretched. She was…protecting me. The outline of my sensors turned from a pale translucent white to a solid flashing red before my eyes. My self-replenishing power core was nearly discharged. All that tuning of my cannon's energy level, all the shots I fired, all the damage I had taken; it was too much. My sensors warned me to temporarily shut down or my systems would fail completely and I would pass out of existence. I couldn't bear to leave Miranda, even though she had nearly killed me…again. I wanted to see what was going to happen, but really, I had no choice. I closed my eyes and tried as best I could to relax, breathing slow and deep. My systems carried this over and forced a shut down. As I was pulled into a coma-like state, my eyes flashed opened and closed and the last thing I saw was Miranda very deliberately draw her blade and hold it out to the side of her, inviting her enemies.

Part VI

How did they get the information they needed so quickly? I imagined our trek was being monitored but how could they have known what I did and how I did it just by watching a security video unless…they were uploading it directly from me. The Commander said battlefield reports when he picked me up from the underground base. But how is it that the signal that may have been coming from me never interfered with any equipment? How is it that Jason couldn't detect it? I ran out of time to follow that train of thought to the next station. I caught the intimation of movement and instantly I ran towards it, grasping my blade with two hands and holding it parallel to my right shoulder, the point protruding out next to my face. When I felt I was near my enemy I jabbed straight out and felt my blade stab through flesh and bone. An awful chocking sound ensued as the cyborg's cloaking device shimmered and deactivated. I had thrust right through his neck. It was no accident that I could somehow picture my enemy, sense him, his movement, even though I couldn't see him. I realized I had sensors too, but they were so deeply embedded into the parts of my brain that controlled my reflexes and housed my natural instincts that they were nearly impossible to notice. The cyborg shook and fell to his knees. At that moment a powerful ball of plasma slammed into my shoulder causing my blade to turn and slice through and out of the neck of the cyborg I had just killed, splashing blood and MR fluids on another nearby cyborg, painting him to the point where he could no longer hide. My cloak shimmered and was gone, disabled by the plasma shot. I backpedaled, expecting another shot. It took me a moment to realize that not only did the shot I just took leave almost no damage but it had barely disrupted my movement and concentration. I glanced over at my shoulder and there wasn't even a mark. I thought it must be the suit. Two more shots blasted out from two unseen foes still well behind the several that were close to me. I took note of their points of origin. I tilted slightly left then right, the shots flying past me, exploding against the far wall. I reached to my belt and drew my knife, flinging it at the cyborg painted with his comrade's blood, hitting him in almost the exact same place I had struck my first victim. I ran up to him as he fell and used my sword to slice off the blade on his arm, picking it up with my other hand and holding each out to one side, ready to unleash a vortex of devastation.

A strange sense of divinity. That pull of the thought of limitless power fills you to the brim with confidence. You feel you would do nothing but good with this power but in the end it leads to your doom. I should have turned away from it but I was tired and weak. For all my strengths I was still human, and humans need to rest. And so there I was, at the borderline of my sanity, the eradication of my humanity on one side, and death on the other. I had to choose.
I pulled both blades in front of me, raised them up over my head and brought them crashing down onto the floor before me; it caved in and formed an empty crest like the inside of a dead volcano. Bubbling up from this perfectly symmetrical hole a palisade of power burst out in front of me and rolled across the room with the force of a tsunami. It seemed to fall across the cyborgs' forms like a sheet pulled onto them. As if taking their very essence, the wall snapped back to reform its original straight axis and the cyborgs power cores, their hearts fused with circuits and microprocessors, were ripped from their bodies all at once along with most of the rest of their half-human organs. They convulsed and collapsed to the floor. The blast wave tore at and dug into the side walls like a thousand claws, slicing off cannon barrels and sending explosions back into their enclosures, roaring all the way to far end of the room where I had emerged and slamming into it at the peak of its momentum, shattering the windows. I

spotted at least 20 forms in each window that ducked for cover. I had already started running. Halfway there, someone in the top left opened window rose up and slapped their hand down on the console in front of them. Gigantic steel shutters crawled up the defenseless gaps. I pushed harder, churned my legs faster. As I neared the far wall I leapt into the air, aiming for the ledge of the top of the door frame. I caught the corner with both hands, placed my feet underneath me and pushed up, tossing myself to the bottom ledge of the bottom left window. I climbed up that, then onto that window's upper ledge. I threw myself up to the bottom ledge of the top window, and as I pulled myself up I heard that familiar terrifying ring. It started in the back of my ears, and grew. Behind my eyes, under my skin, out my ears, all my fear of failure appears. My eyes rose over the ledge already locked with his, the device grasped tightly in his hand, but up for me to see, as if to say 'take it if you can'. It was now or never, but what if I fail? I had left my knife in that cyborg's neck. So many times it was exactly what I needed and now that I needed it more than ever, I didn't have it. Do I risk capture again, crumpling at his feet, an arm's length away from my freedom yet only ensuring my continued servitude? Or can I make it? Grab his hand and crush the device in it before I succumb. Or...do I fall? Let the door close, on what may have well been my only chance, so I could go help a friend. My only friend.

I let go. The ringing subsided, the shutters slammed close, and I hit the ground crouched on one knee with a bang, dust flying up around me. I looked up, then back at where Jason still lay. It felt like it took hours to reach him. I knelt beside him, straightened him up and laid his head against the wall behind him. I placed my hand on his chest and concentrated. I imagined myself in that moment, what it felt like to suddenly understand your true potential, what you were really meant to be. I found it, then I held it all back. I thought

~ 106 ~

of Jason. Of Wheatley and Christiansen, Machae and Jenkins, Stevenson, Givvens...Stafford, Jackson, Mills, O'hara, Lui, Mickelson, Kekoa, Conor...so many names. So many lives in my way. This would not be one more. I channeled the same energy I had felt before into a focused pulse, cylindrical in form and small as the palm of my hand. I pressed it down into Jason. His chest lit up a cold grey-blue, like a low intensity plasma ball. He arched his back and immediately after rose to his feet, like waking up into that place where you're not sure if you're awake or still dreaming. He lifted his cannon and swung it back and forth. I ducked under it as it came around towards me.

"Miranda! You're okay! That's great because what the fuck, why did you just try to kill me!?"

"Jason if I wanted you dead I would have done it by now..."

"Yeah, but do you have to make it hurt so much, I mean...damn..."

"It had to look convincing."

"You know that was more of a rhetorical type of...of question."

"Are you alright?"

"Mentally, or physically? It's okay, don't answer that, I feel like shit in general. But at the same time I feel...stronger. What did you do to me?"

"I'm honestly not really sure."

I didn't want to say too much before I understood more, but it seemed to me that I was controlling some kind of strange frequency; a wavelength that carried no detectable signal yet could produce actual physical force. I couldn't tell if the frequency was just there or if it was coming from me, but it was clear as my hometown sky to me what they were doing. Whatever chips they'd put in me were obviously prototypes; they had no idea what their true potential was. They were engineered that way and they were pushing me, to see if these new micro-wonders they'd created could learn and adapt and improve. As I grew stronger, so did the magnification of that strength through these tiny silicone conductors of my destiny.

"Well, whatever, I'm back, I feel good, let's get going yeah? We need to find a way out of here fast. They won't send any amount of regulars to fight us in such a contained space, but they might be cooking up something else that we don't have the time to deal with right now…so about that door down there…"

Jason turned and lumbered purposefully towards the door, his cannon out and away from his body as he overcharged it.

"Jason, wait, there might be away to deactivate the-"

"No time, I just got finished saying that, now I know you don't listen to me when I talk!"

"That's such bull, I'm always listening, I've been listening since the beginning, that's why you're the only one still alive and with at least *some* of your sanity, parts of it seem to be leaving you."

"I'm…you're right, I'm sorry I…there I go again, see this is what I mean, we don't know how long I'll be able to help you, these chips, these programs and integrations are forcing me to the most direct and aggressive action all the time I…we need to get this door open…now."

I stopped following him. About 8 meters away from the door he halted, raised his cannon, and continued to wait for the strongest charge he could manage. His gun glowed magma red and expanded to nearly twice its original size, looking as if it would blow apart at any moment. He turned his head away and fired, the gun exploding off his arm in a dozen pieces. He stumbled back and broke his fall with his right arm, now the only one he had for the second time. The eruptive hyper-dense sphere roiled and churned and collided with the door, rupturing its superstructure and caving the center inwards. The door remained intact but the middle had been stretched thin and superheated by the blast. It was exactly what I needed. I located my knife and strapped it back onto my belt, then approached the door, sword drawn. I took a heavy downward swipe at the door's weak spot, slicing a hole in it just wide enough to fit my hands through. I put my fingers through the door and pulled the gap open as far as I could, hoping Jason could do the rest once I repaired him. Again. But as I milled over what parts I should use and how exactly I should go about it this time, Jason seemed to read my thoughts yet again and preempted my next action.

"Maybe you should just leave me like this. Or leave me here entirely. I really haven't been much help. I want to be but…if anything I've just gotten in your way so maybe…"

"You still don't get it do you?"

"What do you mean, what don't I get?"

"Everyone's always getting in my way because I don't care. I never gave half a shit about anyone, I just wanted to do what I needed to do and if you couldn't keep up that's too fucking bad. But you're still here. And still I'm attacking you all the time, for my own sake, to save myself. I don't want to be like this anymore. I don't want to think only of myself. I don't want you to go. I can't explain it any more specifically than that. Something inside me has been pulling at me since…maybe since I met you, since we were strapped into that dropship and you looked at me, trying to read my thoughts, like you did so easily just now. I don't know if I'm going to get out of this alive, or with even a shred of what makes me who I am. But if I do, I know that I want you by my side."

"Miranda I…don't do this, fucking look at me! I'm not someone you can just be hanging around with all the time, hell *someone*, some THING is more like it. That chance left along with my body and most of my free will, what do you think should happen to me even if we can make it out together, I'm gonna tag along at your heel like some pet robot!? You know what you *should* do, you should just kill me now and be done with it, put me out of both our miseries!"

"You coward! After all this, you're still here with me and NOW you're gonna give up!? Now, when I'm telling you to your face I need you more than ever!?"

"What do you think this is some kind of fairy tale? *Maybe* one of us *might* get out of this alive, and that one needs to be you, you know that! The best thing that I can do at this point is just stay they hell out of your way. If you won't kill me then at least let me create a diversion, something that will force their attention. I'll use my sensors to find this place's main power generator or something and make a run for it. I'll never get there, but they'll have to send a hell of a lot of stuff after me to stop me, and that's when you can move in on the

Commander. You got any better suggestions, I'd love to hear 'em."

I closed my eyes and suspired in sober surrender. He wasn't wrong. His presence was an increasingly difficult liability. The truth was I had no idea how I was going to make it convincing enough that I had actually killed him at the start of the fight without actually killing him. I was buying myself time, trying to think of a smart way out that would keep us both alive, and get me to Tritium, but really, I didn't know what to do. It was lucky that they decided to unleash their detachment of cyborg clones when they did. I wouldn't be so lucky again. I had left him behind in the underground base. I had tried to kill him, then tried to leave him behind again, and then tried to pretend like I'd killed him and then missed what may have been my only chance to get to the Commander so I could come and help him instead. I wanted to protect him, to keep him safe, to do everything I could to ensure he would survive, but it was only diminishing my ability to finally put a stop to all this. How many impossible choices need I make before I make the last one I will ever need to?

"Okay…Jason. You're right. You're slowing me down. I just…wanted to protect you…"

"I know. But if you don't make it out of here because of me then you'll have done the opposite. You'll have done more harm to me than killing me yourself could ever do. So please…"

"Let me upgrade you again then. I've got a million parts here now and…"

"No time. We've wasted enough talking already. I'll do it myself. You go. And wait for a heightened alert status. This

~ 111 ~

place has been quiet as a tomb unless they were springing traps on us. I'll make it so they'll have to wake up every security system in here and have them all going at the same time. They'll be running around all crazy trying to figure out where I am and how to get rid of me that they'll have to leave you on your own for a while. Then you finish this."

"Okay. I suggest peeling some material off this door to use on your armor. I think you could sacrifice some of your mobility for some extra protection again."

"Okay. Now get going."

I nodded my head and returned my attention to the gap in the door. I looked down at my arms, remembering my cloak had been damaged and rendered unusable. I took off the suit, stripping back down to my under garments, armed with only my knife on my belt, and my new sword in my hand. I looked myself over, at all the scars, scrapes, plasma burns, cuts, cracked skin, dried blood and thought…I was meant for this. The realization of how far I'd come since the underground base, that I felt nothing anymore, was like an arc of lighting flashing across my brain. I had found the perfect balance. I had found someone I wanted to protect, but also the ability to turn off my feelings and face my enemy with no reservations and no remorse. My most arduous challenge lied before me. I turned sideways and slipped through the gap in the door to the other side.

* * * * * * * * * * * *

My first instinct was to find the most intact dead cyborg and switch bodies with him. Incredibly risky for sure. I may not survive the transfer. But it would take me hours, perhaps even a whole day to refine this mostly broken form into something that could pose a real threat to their creations. If one of the cyborgs was mostly undamaged I could perhaps spend only a handful of hours retrofitting some extra armor plating, fine tuning my sensors, and be ready to go. As I searched the bodies I came across one that had his neck sliced open by Miranda but was otherwise untouched. I dragged the body over to the nearest wall and propped it up into a sitting position. I sat down cross-legged in front of it and slowly pulled its helmet off. Givvens. One of my best friends for years lay before me, lifeless and desecrated. I pulled my helmet off to look at him with my own eyes. I felt a very human lump in my throat. My lips dried, my head ached, and my eyes watered. I punched the ground repeatedly. I looked around the room at the dozen or so other bodies, wondering which one was Stevenson, deciding it was best I didn't look. 'I'm sorry Todd' I said to myself as I found his chest seal and pulled on the side of his suit, opening it like a washing machine door. I carefully lifted his body out and laid it gently on the ground, crossed his arms over his chest and slid his eyes shut. I began powering down my systems, and peeling myself out of my prison of steel and circuits. At last I was free. I flopped to the floor like a worm, naked as the day I was born into a pool of blood and MR fluids, barely able to move or even breathe. One-armed, I dragged myself across the cold sanguineous floor and into Givven's suit, pulling the chest plate closed.

As my systems powered up, I could tell they were nearly identical to the way Miranda had coded and colligated my microchips in conjunction with my brain. Aside from a handful of amateurish hacks and re-routes, everything was set up like it was in my own suit. They must have been downloading data directly from her thought processes, which means they probably had more control over her than they had exerted so far. Maybe they felt she was more effective without interference, or perhaps they feared damaging her.

She was so smart and so capable that they were using her to strengthen the army I'm certain she was meant to lead, then testing it out on her to see how it measured up. I was no one in all this, not even a small piece of the puzzle; just an expendable vessel to see if the real pieces would fit. Therein lay my advantage. They would have abandon surveillance of this room, moving their officer corps elsewhere, and concentrating on pinpointing Miranda's location. I could slip away unnoticed and get to somewhere I might pose an actual threat. The cloak on Givven's suit wasn't functioning either, but I figured that was best. I wouldn't be tempted to hide. I could always try to reroute power later and possibly force it into action. I decided to focus on upgrading my armor plating as Miranda had suggested. I used my blade to slice off thin pieces of the still heated door and patch-welded them onto myself with the heat exhaust from my cannon. After a few hours I was in the best shape I was going to get without a proper set of tools. I didn't want to go the same way Miranda went and though I knew they were long gone, I decided my best bet was to find a way in through those sealed slats and see where that led. I examined the blade underneath my cannon and sure enough, it was hinged. I locked it into its right-angle position, approached the wall, jumped up and jammed the blade through as high as I could. I pulled myself up on it and grabbed onto the bottom ledge of the bottom right slat. I pulled myself into the windowsill, hanging onto the top ledge. I tuned my cannon for a moderate shot and blasted the steel shutter at point blank range. The smoke cleared and there was a hole just big enough for me to squeeze through with some effort. On the other side were 5 rows of consoles, still flashing and beeping. I walked down the first row, examining the monitors. Some displayed encounter outcome projections; some showed biometric classifications of our team, including Miranda and myself. Anatomic specifications, battlefield data analysis programs, microchip diagrams, genome charts, the works. They hadn't expected whatever Miranda had done while I was unconscious and they certainly didn't expect me to still be around.

The tide was turning. No longer were our enemies omnipresent puppet masters; they had left traces of their plans, however slight, and I could take them. I placed my empty hand near what looked like a touch screen next to one of the monitors. My systems linked up to the mainframe and automatically initiated a hacking protocol almost identical to what Miranda had us do in the underground base. In just a few minutes the overlay of my sensors on my eyes flashed a bright green and began downloading thousands of files in groups of hundreds at a time. As I did, the monitors around me began flashing rapidly and shutting down. The system was trying to cut me off, but Miranda's enhancements, that they themselves copied, were beyond their own core system's ability to contend with. I retrieved every last bit of data just before the room went dark. I tried sifting through it briefly but there was so much information I quickly became overwhelmed and confused. A single piece of data stuck out: 'Stevenson, Gary. Corporal, Spec Ops Delta, 1st Platoon – Advance to Project Eldritch'. So Stevenson was still alive. I hoped I didn't run into him, especially in whatever terrible form he would likely take coming out of a project with a name like that. Behind the last row of monitors was the blurry outline of a sealed door. I figured I needed some light anyway so I turned my cannon to near maximum charge and fired, blasting the door to dust. The outline of my shot that had finished its push well past the door pulsed a deep red and I followed it out of the room and through several walls. Finally the breaches ceased and I was faced with a choice. I could go left or right down all too familiar looking corridors, or I could try blasting through more walls to see how far I could get. That sounded like more fun. I took a few steps back and fired another powerful blast into the wall before me. I could tell that whatever Miranda had done to awaken me had carried over. It wasn't part of my suit, perhaps not even a part of my computerized enhancements, but part of me. Again, a dozen or more red rings led me onward. This place was absolutely enormous. 3 more times I blasted my way forward, constantly expecting a reinforced section to halt my progress and force me sideways. But it didn't happen. Miranda would need heavy weaponry to do this but they obviously weren't prepared for anyone like me to be here.

I came to a wall that looked different form the others. It was a rust red-color, instead of the cold smokey black-grey of nearly every section preceding it. It seemed considerably thicker and denser, but not impenetrable. I decided to try a different approach. I searched along the wall for a console and found one about 30 meters to the right. Just like the consoles in the room before, it had a touch panel next to the monitor. I placed my hand on it and my systems started another, different hacking protocol; this one seemingly designed to break a digital combination lock. It took much longer. Several times I pulled my hand away when my sensors flashed an intimidating red, guessing it was probably some security measure trying to lock me out. My system would pick up where it left off. Suddenly the entire wall shuddered and began sliding away from me. The floor I was standing on shook and shifted up and out through the colossal set of doors as they peeled open. Before me was a hangar that stretched out farther than I could see. Though there was light pouring down from the ceiling, the illumination didn't get far enough down for me to see what was below. As my eyes and sensors adjusted, and as the platform I was on sank down towards the floor, rows upon rows of cyborgs came into view. They were all inactive, hunched over and motionless, lined up in perfect formation, facing off to my left. The platform touched down and I stepped off. Had there been any active security systems in the area I would have been easily caught off guard as I gaped at the sight before me. There were thousands. Maybe tens of thousands; I couldn't see the end of the chamber from where I was. It was a manufactured, mass produced army of the dead, wrenched back into existence to relive as killers, only this time without pity or remorse or reason. Only the inscrutable and wicked whims of their masters would drive them, to whatever end. My first instinct was to destroy each and every last one of them, but I could risk activating them and be easily overwhelmed, or end up altering their masters before I could do much damage. I walked to the wall on my far right and proceeded along it, searching for an exit. I saw a door not 10 meters away but before I could get there, a low pitched rumble and several deep and thunderous booms echoed through the hangar. I looked where it seemed the sound was coming from, behind and above me on the opposite side of the hangar. I could discern scaffolding running the length of the hanger, similar to the one I had ridden down on, but considerably smaller and much higher up. A gigantic ball of orange and blue fire erupted from the far dark corner, chunks of metal flying into the air. Another explosion, then another, and another, each slightly larger than the last, following each other deeper and deeper into the room, closer and closer to me. My sensors began flashing that foreboding bright red and focused my vision on Miranda; she was sprinting across the scaffolds, just ahead of the explosions, her knife and her sword stretched out behind her like wings. I froze; she was so far ahead of me already. I never even had a chance to do anything. I was foolish to think I could. But then, I knew that most of what I said was just to get her away from me, so I wouldn't slow her down anymore. At least that part seemed to have worked. However long it took me to upgrade myself was all the time she needed. I heard the sound of large steel doors grinding open, the same sound the ones that unleashed Miranda on me before had made. A faint light shown at the far end of the hangar. Suddenly, hundreds of active cyborgs egressed from the darkness, their cannons aimed at me. My first instinct was to turn and run but I thought I could perhaps buy Miranda some time to escape from whatever she was trying to get away from. As the cyborgs approached, some broke off into the ranks of the dormant ones and started powering them up, dozens of burning red-orange eyes lighting up at a time, all turning towards me. I changed my cannon to moderate intensity and started firing as quickly and accurately as I could, aiming for shoulders and knees and helmets. I knew I wouldn't be able to focus my attacks on any one cyborg long enough to kill them before the others engulfed me, but I could keep many of them at bay. One of my shots connected with a cyborg's shoulder, knocking him back, another hit another's knee, causing him to stumble forward and nearly fall. Another shot smacked right into one of the cyborg's helmet's, knocking it clean off. When the beast righted itself, I could clearly see my friend, Frank Machae, his face pale and ghastly, eyes once so vibrant replaced by windows into hell. Not even him had they spared. They must have been only a few kilometers behind us and had picked him up almost immediately after we scattered and passed out of sight. I called out to him but it was no use. Miranda had truly saved me. Had they taken me any other way they would have killed me and stripped me of every last drop of life and stuck me into this shell as nothing more than an organic machine. Miranda had left me the chance to hold onto my humanity, or die with it. The other cyborgs own plasma blasts started streaking dangerously close to me. Several struck my armor and though it held, I had lost my advantage. I turned and started to sprint away but just as I faced forward, Miranda dropped down in front of me, crouched on one knee, smacking into the ground with such force it cracked beneath her. She whipped her head up and gave me a sight I was not at all prepared for. Her corneas crackled and glowed with an electric-like current, blue and purple and white, spindles of light churning and rotating around her irises. 'Move', she says to me, a tone as flat and sharp as her blade. I backpedaled and pinned myself up against the wall, and if you had seen my face it would have portrayed nothing but crippling dread. I thought of my defiled and embarrassing state, wondering if I could ever live outside of this walking casket and feel like a person again. I should have been watching the cyborgs in case one of them tried to take a shot at me or charge, but I could only stare wide-eyed and horrified at Miranda, wondering if she was still human. If she still had a heart that could still be mine.

Part VII

They only imagined they had unleashed me before. They had no idea what they made me capable of. The forces they were tampering with lied far outside their realm of comprehension and only now was it beginning to crystalize in their minds; only now were they beginning to see just how far out of their reach I was…had always been. I wasn't falling deeper into their control. I was pulling further away, each battle an increasingly dramatic movement toward my freedom. They had me cornered, locked between a proverbial rock and a hard place. Commander Tritium stood before me, easily within striking distance, the grey single-button remote gripped firmly in his hand. He tossed me a black one-piece form-fit personalized combat suit, thin and skin tight but flexible and strong as steel. No cloak this time; he didn't want his goddess vanishing on him again. He told me he knew what I sought, and that he alone could give it to me. He alone held all the answers to all the questions. What really happened to the world to bring about this downfallen and delirious state? Who are the Black Hand? What am I? Why me? He told me he could restore Jason, bring him back close to his former self, and that we could be together. I believed him for a few fleeting seconds. Not because I thought he was telling the truth, but because I needed to.

He pressed the button down hard and sent me into a tortured convulsion, his cyborg guards bearing down on me, to capture me yet again and stick me at the bottom of some other mind bending maze of violence with the illusion of choice. But then something happened they did not anticipate. This man with his speeches and his answers was at last rendered mute and could only stare aghast at my equally silent transformation. The innocent and naïve little girl of my past met face to face with the surreptitious slayer, that taker of hopes and dreams, and stared her down to the ground to cower at the purity of her perception, the truth of her heart. No longer could I keep these two contradicting halves of myself mutually exclusive. For the first time in my life they existed in the same place at the same time, causing a spiritual explosion that shook the very foundations of my being. I knew what it meant to sacrifice, to give up all of yourself in order to save someone else, and to want nothing more than to let go of your life so that they would have one more handle with which to pull themselves up and out of despair. That's how you matter. That's how you make a difference. Jason was my microcosm of what I wanted for the world, my only home. The part of myself that still had hope for humanity, that I had always been saving for the day I might be free of the need to kill, had already won. Yet the need to kill remained. Entirely new conduits of communication between the highly advanced microchips embedded in my brain spread out before me, like water poured onto what seemed to be a smooth surface but proved to be filled with thousands of tiny creases and crevasses, trailing off in countless directions and finding pathways never before conceptualized. I saw and understood the world around me as if I had lived for lifetimes and seen the outcomes of a million choices, and everything those choices affected. I could feel not just my own energy, but that of the walls and the air, and even my enemies. Then I realized that energy was at my command. I grasped as much of it as my hands could hold and cast it back at them, a wave of their own malice and indifference, magnified and personified by my rage. The force rippled through the air and blasted the cyborgs to pieces. The Commander stood singed but unharmed and found the remote was now nothing more than a mound of dust in his hand. More than that, I could feel the once ever-present pressure of his will had vanished. 'I am your goddess of death no longer', I said to him, and I ran, making my way back through the endless corridors to look for Jason.

When I found him I could think of nothing else save how much I had wronged him. Of how monumentally I had failed him because I could not reconcile myself sooner. He paid the price for my procrastination, suffered for my shillyshally, and all I could do for him now was rain more destruction and death. And so it rained. Like so many times before I charged headlong into my enemies. I pushed so much energy into the ground that it broke into pieces and flew apart and away from me. I lifted off the ground as if leaping, my left leg straight, my right bent slightly at the knee. In one motion I covered 10 meters and was on top of the dozen or so closest cyborgs to me. I smashed into one that was right in front of me with my shoulder, then spun and cleaved his head clean off, the shockwave from my slice covering 360 degrees around me and causing the other cyborgs to stumble backwards. As my feet touched the ground, I twisted my torso and brandished my sword from right to left in a wide arc, sending out a similar shockwave that slammed into several cyborgs with such force that their armor broke apart and they fell to the ground incapacitated. Cyborgs from my right started taking shots at me. I stuck my knife in my belt and with my right hand outstretched I projected an inverted static shockwave that hung in the air, a shield wielding itself, oscillating at an alien frequency. The blasts of plasma sploshed against the barrier like balls of blown glass filled with liquid shattering against a slab of solid ice. Several cyborgs kept firing as several more approached me, their blades stretched out in front of them. I brought my left hand back and pushed into the inverted wave, collapsing it outward and closing it down onto the advancing cyborgs, crushing them as if under a massive hydraulic press and sending a clap of force fluxing forward and crashing into several more cyborgs like a tidal wave, pushing them down and back. Immediately, 20 something more blasts of plasma came flying towards me. I ducked and spun, jumped and twisted, turned and twirled and every single shot missed. I surveyed the battleground and

~ 122 ~

reevaluated my situation. Cyborgs were activating and advancing faster than I could kill them. I couldn't keep up these kinds of attacks forever and soon I would be overwhelmed.

I snapped my stare to Jason, still frozen in awe. I ran to him, wrapped my right arm around his back, spun, and launched him some 40 meters to the platform it seemed he had ridden down on to get here. He nearly fell forward but caught himself on a side railing. Sensing a cyborg was right behind me I ducked down under his thrusting blade and spun around, slicing his legs off at the knees. I took two steps back and then slammed my sword blade first into the ground, initiating a rolling wall of power that curled up the floor and collided with several hundred cyborgs, knocking them over and up and into still more cyborgs. I took a few deep breaths then ran towards the platform. Jason, aware again, was already launching low-intensity plasma shots into the cyborgs disoriented ranks, causing puffs of blue mist and a rain of sparks as they cooled, blanketing the battlefield in a murky fog. I reached the platform, scrambled for a control panel and found a very small touch screen towards the middle. A button read "Retract". The second I hit it, the platform lurched and rose. As we cleared the blue mist, cyborgs father back in the ranks started firing, but they were too far to retain any accuracy and the shots splattered around us randomly. I could feel Jason's eyes fixed on me, unblinking and unbelieving.

"How…what...where did…when…who are you?"

"You forgot why…"

"Oh…that's real funny Miranda, just goddamn hilarious WHAT THE FUCK WAS THAT!? This is impossible, you have like fucking superpowers now, where did this come from, how did you…"

"Could you relax please!? I thought you were a soldier? Microchips or no, you need to pull yourself the fuck together Sergeant, that's an order!"

"Y-yes ma'am…Lieutenant. But…what exactly happened to you since we separated?"

"A story for another time. Right now all that we need to think about is getting the hell out of this place. I think we're close to the exit."

"What gives you that impression? I mean besides your superpowers…"

I tilted my head and glared at Jason playfully; ever the quipster, always looking for every chance to say something silly. And every time he did I felt my heart lift just a little. It reminded me that what made Jason the man that leant me all his strength so that I could press on without even meaning to was still there. There was still time.

"The Commander. He put himself in harm's way. Was standing three meters in front of me. He took a huge risk that could have gotten him killed. I don't believe there's any way he would have taken that chance had I not been close to escaping. We have to find an alternate route back to where I was when I destroyed his remote."

"Wait, you destroyed the remote!? Then…then you're free!"

"The remote was never really the issue. I can safely say I'm not his slave anymore...but we're not out of this yet."

"So what's the plan LT?"

I smiled, even chuckled a little. Just like old times, not so long ago. It was good to be together again. This time only death would part us.

"This place seems to have been built like a grid, in that you can get to any corridor form any other corridor, though we may have to take some circuitous directions. There's more than one way to get to the room I was in; we just need to find it. I came to it from a westerly course so we're going to try an easterly one…that way."

I pointed to our right at a corridor just coming into view as the platform reached its summit and locked itself in place.

"Yeah, that's where I was gonna go next but I got sidetracked by the strangeness of this wall."

Jason pointed to the left where half of the wall was closing in towards us. I looked back to the right, then closed my eyes and focused my mind. I could picture the path as if I was speeding through, following its straightways and its sharp turns, dozens of directions changes, ultimately leading to a door at the right of the room where I had entered on the left and faced Tritium. That must be it. The last room. And beyond it…freedom. But I could not see past it. Something was blocking my senses, but what? Or who? As soon as the wall finished closing I made my way down the right corridor and motioned for Jason to follow. Turn after turn I followed my instincts, all the while the walls themselves shuddering from the thousands of cyborgs that were flooding the maze, trying to cut us off. We reached a door not unlike the one that had led us in here, its inner workings on display, daring us to find a way through. But I knew the fastest way.

"TRITIUM! I know you're there! I know you can hear me you coward! Not once have you told me the truth and you thought I would just…wilt like a dying flower!? Bend to your will out of desperation or guilt or blindness!? I will NEVER submit! You'll have to kill me which means this demented little pet project of yours will have failed, so you may as well let me go so I can make an actual difference somewhere, instead of just running around in this maze picking apart your army till you have nothing left!"

A voice echoed through the corridor, but it seemed to be coming not from some loudspeaker or PA system, but from the walls and the floor and ceiling, pushing into my ears and coming out of them at the same time.

"Hahahahahahaha! All I ever needed was you. No, not you, but your spirit…the driving force behind what makes you so impossible to control. I needed to know that spirit could be tapped, accessed, exploited…turned into a weapon. And you have become a most formidable weapon…"

The door before us hissed and popped. Steam poured out from the edges and slowly it lurched open outwards.

"You are but a handful of choices away from what you seek."

The voice fell silent and seemed to physically leave my ears. I turned to Jason.

"I'm with you LT. Whatever you wanna do…"

"Step through the door with me but hang back, give me a 30 second head start."

The room was about half the size of the arena where I had battled Jason and his clones. Not huge, but there was enough space that making a break for the exit would likely not be viable depending on what Tritium had waiting for us. I stepped through the door and Jason followed, pausing just inside as I had asked him to. I walked slowly, my eyes fixed forward but my ears searching for the slightest sound or vibration. There was nothing. I got a little more than half way across the room when glaring floodlights nearly blinded me and I could hear the footsteps of a hundred heavily armed soldiers marching in and around me. My eyes adjusted and I was surrounded, all of them carrying high-intensity plasma rifles trained on me. Several more had cornered Jason and he remained still, waiting. In a suit similar to the one he had given me and draped in a long beige overcoat, Tritium stood in stoic silence but something was different about him this time. Always he had been a sinister shadow over my every attempt to break free, to uncover the truth; always this predominating presence that, no matter how close I thought I was getting, would always slam the door in my face and force me back into my dungeon of deprivation to lose a little bit more of my soul trying to find the way out. Yet through all this he had always been just a man, his specter a consequence of his power over me, not of his own power. But as he stood there I felt a subliminal surge, a mounting mutating malevolence that was taking physical form, much like my resolution had when just last we had met. He strolled towards me, arms crossed behind his back, his gait calm and confident. When he was close enough I could make out a faint electric-like glow in his eyes.

"You were my prototype Miranda…my paradigm, a window a thousand years into the future of what mankind was capable of gifting himself. I needed to know if my theory was true. If the most powerful force on the battlefield was not the weapon in the soldiers hand, or even the soldier himself, but the reason behind why they carried that weapon, *why* they fought. I needed someone whose reason was greater than them, greater than all the world. I always felt we were not so different you and I. And now…I am certain of it."

In an instant he was inside my guard, his movement a gauzy blurr. I was so startled that I couldn't react in time. He reached back and slammed his fist into the side of my face, lifting me off my feet and sending me floating up and back, my sword dropping out of my hand. It felt long enough for a good night's rest before I hit the ground and skid across it, nearly to where we had entered. Before I could stand he was on me again. He lifted his left leg up and brought his heel down towards my chest, but I rolled out of the way. Anticipating this, he was already half way down with his right hand, aiming for the spot I rolled into. I caught his fist in both my hands, barely able to stop it from plowing right through and putting a hole in my chest. He grabbed me by the shoulders and lifted me up, then let go, spun and kicked into my chest, sending me flying into the wall; my arms and legs splaying against it as I slid down. He charged, his face expressionless, his right arm cocked back, fist clenched tight. It would have been my end. Just before he struck , a plasma blast hit him on his left cheek, jerking his head around and sending him tumbling over himself and splatting onto the ground. Before I could even look to see where Jason was, a cacophony of gunfire erupted and I ran up the center of the room with all the speed I could muster, the zipping sound of bullets all around me. I picked up my sword where it had fallen and began cutting and slicing at any enemy I could reach, severing limbs, chopping bodies in half, decapitating and decimating. I caught sight of Jason. He blasted off bursts of plasma and thrashed about with his blade and his fist, his enemies' attacks bouncing off him or missing him entirely as he countered and contorted, shot and struck and stabbed and slashed. More and more of the soldiers focused their attention on him.

Tritium rose slowly, wiping himself off and cracking his neck. This time I was ready for him. With what seemed like even more celerity, he was on me in a second. I swung my blade up from the floor, but he spun out of the way, finishing his spin with a roundhouse kick aimed at my head. I ducked down and moved forward and around him, then lunged straight out. He leaned sideways, my blade stabbing through his coat, but missing his flesh. He spun towards me and struck my sword at its center with both his palms, knocking it out of my hand. Even as I felt the impact of his attack I was reaching for my knife with my other hand. He thought he would be fast enough to connect with a right jab before I could bring up my knife but I beat him to his punch, shoving the knife through the bottom of his wrist, the tip popping out of the top of his arm. He barely flinched, leaning into a powerful front kick to my abdomen that sent me stumbling backwards and away from him, my knife still stuck in his arm. He joggled it lose and yanked it out, blood pouring out from the wound, but still he only winced slightly, a sickening smile growing across his half-charred face as he tossed my knife to the ground beside him.

"Hahaha you SEE! You thought you were special but this power is in everyone! You just have to want it enough and stick a few microchips in your brain to give it form and function. I was afraid the effects of using it might kill me, but when I saw you unleash it with such ease and grace, such rage…I knew that using it would only make me stronger."

"But I don't understand, what do you need this power for? And why give it to me?"

"Why I need it for the same reason you do! To make a difference. To force the change I see best for this unkept and disrespected world. Those is power seek to keep it but I will take it from them."

"By employing more violence, more death!?"

"You are no different, oh goddess no longer. All you've done to find your way is kill, murder, destroy. You know nothing else. That's why I gave it to you. I knew you would stop at nothing to achieve your goal, reach the destiny you believed was meant for you. I wanted to see this unbridled passion in all its vestal resplendency. And what a beautiful sight it is. Now I know its potential. Now I can unleash my own destiny upon the world and take it where *I* want it to go. And yet…you still have a chance to save yourself and your friend Miranda. Join me. Together we will make of this world what it *should* be, what *we* desire!"

"I want no part of whatever you desire Tritium. There's nothing you can do to help anyone. Only yourself."

"If that is your choice then I don't need you anymore. You'll just get in my way. So you, like so many that stood in *your* way, must die!"

He charged again, his feet pounding into the ground, cracking it with each step. He cocked his right arm back, fist clenched tight. I waited until the last possible second then leaned out to my right and tried to grab his now outstretched arm. Just as I placed my hand on him, he grabbed my arm and stomped down on my left foot, pinning me in place, then bashed his forehead into mine. I had never been so disoriented. For the first time I was completely unaware, unable to detect where the next attack was coming from, or what I should do to try and stop it. He lifted me up over his head with both hands and tossed me halfway across the room. I plowed into the metal floor, curling it up as if it were dirt, grinding to a stop amidst a semicircle of soldiers. I made a feeble attempt to right myself but my hands failed to find good placement, my arms shook, and I fell prostrate. I looked up expecting to see my nemesis looming over me, ready to deliver the final blow but what I saw instead I could not at first understand. Tritium was stiff, frozen in place, his arms close to his sides, his teeth clenched, his eyes darting back and forth. A familiar shimmer behind him revealed Jason, his free arm wrapped tightly around the Commander's body, his blade pressed against his neck.

"Let her go or I'll turn this guy into a pez dispenser before you can fire your first shot!"

Jason tightened his grip and pulled his blade even harder, drawing blood. The Commander gave his order.

"Do it!"

The soldiers lowered their weapons and I stood slowly, wobbling and holding my head. The soldiers backed away and Tritium spoke.

"Now what fools!?"

"Miranda! Come, come here!"

I walked to Jason's side, retrieving my sword and my trusty knife along the way. I looked up at his still hulking form, through his mask, past the pale skin and veins and computer enhanced brain functions, past the brave young man the military had made out of him...and saw my other half. My better half. Jason could have killed him then and there. I was hurt, but no amount of regular soldiers would have a chance against me. With their guards down I would have slaughtered them all. But he didn't. All this time I was so certain I had been holding onto my humanity, but despite my revelation, I was only slipping further away from the only thing I ever really needed to hold onto. My past self had given me lucidity and unity of vision but I had used it only to create more death. Jason had just saved my life and had done so without taking our most dangerous enemy's in reciprocation. Perhaps I had been wrong about myself all along. Perhaps Tritium knew me better than I knew myself.

"Now these 'fools' are gonna walk out of here with YOU, and no one is gonna stop us! Right!?"

"Whatever you say boy. You haven't the slightest idea what you're doing."

Jason started walking backwards with Tritium in tow. I turned and located a door at the far end of the room, running my hands along the frame and nearby walls searching for a control panel. My subtle sensors picked up an equally elusive hidden touch screen, covered by a metal panel on the wall just to the center-right of the door. I used my fingers to lift the cover and placed my hand on the screen. The microchips in my brain were able to decode the pass sequence and transmit the necessary data to my fingertips. A tiny pulse of energy flowed through them and the panel shorted out, opening the door and rendering the panel useless. Sunlight swarmed in through the opening. We stepped through and I jumped up and pulled the door down, slamming it to the floor. It stayed closed. We turned to find ourselves in a hangar similar to where the army of cyborgs had been slumbering, but this one was cut off, the far end opening up to vast woodland of bamboo, palm and fig trees, with majestic Kapoks punctuating the landscape, towering over the rest of the flora. Off in the distance I could see small flocks of dark birds flitting from tree top to tree top as they swayed almost indiscernibly in a gentle breeze I was dying to feel, over a lithesome waterfall I was dying to drink from. I began to sense the freedom I had been fighting so hard for so long to possess. I almost wandered off into the jungle when Jason called to me.

"Hey! So what the hell do we do with this guy? I move a quarter inch the wrong way and he breaks free and probably kills us both."

"Indeed I will."

"I…we should…"

"HAHAHAHA NOW you have an attack of conscience!? Now you show weakness? This is why you could NEVER reach your destiny, why it HAS to be ME!"

"Miranda I don't think I can hold him much longer. Hell I don't even know if slicing his throat will kill him so whatever you're gonna do, do it fast!"

I looked down and put my hand to my forehead, breathing hard and heavy, my emotions bouncing between contempt and regret, fear and rage, pity and justness. Where was my notion of the clarity of right and wrong now? Why could I not see what it was I should do, even what I wanted to do. I looked up. He was holding Jason off the ground by his neck in one hand and smiling that maniacal smile at me.

"Too late!"

He pulled back and punched clean through Jason's chest. In his hand was Jason's power core; his heart, physically half-human, yet more so than mine. He tossed him aside, throwing Jason's own heart at his limp body.

"You know I really thought he was dead the first time. And then I thought I could turn him but he proved to be a strong one-well…not strong enough."

"You…you demon! You soulless monster you don't deserve to live never mind achieve the end of any path you may have chosen! I don't care how strong you think you are, DIE NOW!"

In one motion I threw down my sword, drew my knife to my left hand and sprang into the air, bearing down on him with a courageous verve so present and powerful that a cone of blue-white energy formed before me. Tritium held his left arm up to his face and stretched out his right as if to grab me. The cone of energy dug into his guarding arm and pushed him down to one knee. I came down on him knife first but he caught my attacking hand with his right and flipped me over him. I landed on the ground with so much force that he lost his balance and had to catch himself from falling over. I took a step forward and struck down hard with my free hand, fist clenched so tight I couldn't feel my own fingers, my knuckles colliding with his jaw. His head jerked but his stance remained solid. I threw my knee up into his chin and simultaneously chopped downward with my right hand, his head moved up into my strike as it connected with the back of his neck. He buckled and nearly fell, barely holding himself up off the ground. I turned away from him and whipped myself into a handstand, kicking up at his neck and flipping him over onto his back. He handsprung up and went for a strong left cross, but I spun around his strike, wrapped my knife-wielding arm around his head, dropped and pulled him down with me, slamming his head into the ground. He reached over my chest with his left arm and pinned me for a moment, then tried to climb on top of me. I rolled backwards and over, pinning him instead, then raised my left hand. He deflected my strike but the ruse had worked. I had switched my knife from my left hand to my right. I jabbed into his side and he cried out, grabbing my arm as my blade dug into him. With his left he threw a strong hook to my face and knocked me off him but I kept my knife this time. I rolled off, caught myself with my now free left hand, then spun back towards him, stabbing and slashing with my knife, lashing out with my fist, my left leg, my knife again, a right roundhouse, and left cross, a right side kick, another swipe with my knife. Tritium ducked and dodged and shifted and swerved, blocking and evading every one of my attacks with so much speed I could barely keep up my assault. Then I looked in his eyes and saw fear. I took hold of it with all of my aching heart and pulled it close to me. I made his fear my own and showed him that despite all he might do there was no escaping yourself, no way to erase the dread of failure; accepting that you will was the only way to give all of yourself, with no remorse, and nothing held back. He had restrained himself out of fear that he would be pushed to his limits and still lose and in doing so had given me enough time to bring that fear to the forefront and use it against him. I reached down inside myself and tore from my own being every ounce of energy and passion I had in me, from the day I could dream till now and heaped it onto my onslaught. With every strike he took a step back, and every few steps his knees weakened. I wheeled him around with his back towards the hangar's opening, pushing him nearly to the edge when he ascertained my timing and caught my knife-wielding wrist in one hand, and my fist in the other. I planted my feet and pushed down on his arms, bending his knees nearly to the ground as he shook with impotence.

"How…can this be!?"

He fell to his knees and in in two quick motions I snapped both of his forearms and they fell limp to his sides as his scream echoed out into the forest.

"All you have is your hatred."

"It isn't ture! I have a vision, a dream, a path set before me clear as this view! I'm faster than you, stronger than you...how did you beat me?"

"Because I have something you don't..."

Tritium's mouth hung open, his eyes quivering, running a thousand possibilities through his mind, light years away from the only answer.

"Someone else to fight for."

And with all my strength I shoved my knife into his heart, grabbed his head with both hands and violently turned his eyes to the trees, then kicked him off the edge and down to the undergrowth for the earth to reclaim him. Panting heavily I ran back to the hangar's only door where Jason, barely alive, had dragged himself up against.

"Oh Jason, it's my fault I should have just finished him when you gave me the chance I'm sorry I'm so sorry! "

Burning tears cut through the dirt and grime and dried blood on my face like lava leaking from a volcano that had just killed itself with its final explosion. I didn't know if there was even one more battle, one more strike left in me, watching Jason fade into darkness right in front of me. And there was nothing I could do. With heaving breaths every few words he spoke, his voice raspy and weak.

"It's okay Miranda...you did the right thing...it's the only difference...between you and him...but it's all the difference...in the world..."

"No! No, YOU are all the difference in my world! It's only because of you I made it this far, only because of you that I survived. Even while this body was trying to drag you into slavery you fought, you resisted, and you made me strong enough to face myself, my fears. And when that wasn't enough you *saved* me! Not just my life, but who I am! I'm nothing, I'm no one, I don't exist without you!"

Jason's eyes started to flutter, each blink longer than the last. His breath grew calmer and shorter and his muscles relaxed. He sighed.

"That's...sweet of you to say. But you'll always have me with you..."

Jason held up his power core. The shape and some tissue remained, but most of it was wires and circuits and power cells and microchips. I wanted to take my knife and tear them all out of my brain and die by his side. His hand fell to the ground as his eyes blinked closed and didn't open again.

"Jason! Please don't go I need you I don't...know where to go or or what to do! You have to help me you have to stay with me please don't go!..I love you!"

I clenched his hand in both of mine and sobbed.

****

I awoke with a quake and a gasp, for a moment thinking that it had all just been a horrible nightmare. I stared out over the jungle. The sun was just coming up over the horizon spilling silky golden bands of light over the treetops. Jason lay next to me silent, serene…at peace. I looked down at my hand. I was still holding his heart. I knew the cyborgs were looking for another way out, but with Tritium gone they were likely disoriented. Perhaps they had even turned on the soldiers guarding the base. Yet I felt no need to rush. I placed Jason's heart down beside him, then pulled open his suit and removed his lifeless body. I carried him to the hangar's edge and looked at him one last time. I was sure he hadn't been smiling when I picked him up, but now he was. I let him go, down into the forest, probably not far from where Tritium himself lay. Two fallen soldiers. In another time, another life, they might have been comrades; brothers in arms defending the world from the ache I had only been intensifying. I walked back to where I'd placed Jason's heart. I thought hard about the last thing he said to me. Jason was never one to speak in riddles but something was telling me that because he had so little time left he needed to tell me something he knew I would not simply take at face value, that I would think about and could do something with. I started slowly pulling out wires and peeling off circuitry until I came across a very different looking microchip. Whereas the others were square and flat, no bigger than half a pinky finger nail, this one was oval, had girth, and was half a thumb long. It pulsed a deep blue from within. As I held it between my fingers, the chip lit up and sent lines of bright blue light down my hand, up my arm, across my chest and, I guessed, into my head. My ever present but never recognizable sensors finally showed themselves. Wherever my eyes looked I could obtain information and was given a detailed written readout. I looked at the metal floor and knew what it was made of, at the door and saw through it, and how to go around it. I looked out at the forest and saw what every type of tree was, how tall and how old they were, and how far way. Markers indicated where the nearest signs of movement and life were, as well as nearby computer systems, and how to access their networks. I felt as if my half-blind stumble through every situation I found myself in would henceforth be a calculated tactical advance on my enemies. I had only to imagine myself seeing as any other person would and suddenly the overlay fell away and I looked upon the world with my own eyes again. Just as I did, a small window flashed before my sight showing a rectangular box with a wavelength meter across it. The meter jumped and rippled as Jason's voice awoke in my ears.

"Hi Miranda. If you're hearing this, and I know you will, then Tritium is dead and most likely rotting at the bottom of the forest…along with me. There was…so much I wanted to say to you. It's my fault for arghhhh never having the courage to do it. And now it's too late. Well, almost. I love you Miranda. You're the strongest, most beautiful, most intelligent, most focused and determined person I've ever known. You're skill in battle is matched only by…uhhhh…your bravery. And yet you have such a gentle, caring way when you want to. You tell me I saved you but…you saved me first. I would have given up if not for you, but I had the chance to help you and…my only regret is that I can't help you anymore. Except for this; the microchip you hold is similar to the ones you have in you, as far as I can tell but newer, more advanced. I imprinted some information on it, files I downloaded from their computer systems, combat data from my battles and a few other things, but I can't access its core database. It seems every cyborg was implanted with one of these but none of us could unlock its true potential. Only you can do that. So now it's up to you. There are a lot of choices you're going to have to make…and you'll have to make all of them on your own. But I will be here with you…always. Goodbye Miranda. You were never anyone's goddess…but mine."

I felt a lake of tears forming behind my eyes by my dam of determination held. I unzipped the top of my suit and pulled down my bra enough to get to the skin over my heart. I took my knife and cut into my chest, my hand shaking slightly. Once I had made a complete circle, I dug out a chunk of flesh. I placed the microchip in the wound, and used the tip of my knife to press it up against my heart. Sure enough it latched onto the tissue and sent a shock of energy through my body. I felt stronger than ever, but whatever darker secrets it held would have to wait. I found some cloth I had torn off Tritium's jacket in our fight and made a patch out of it, holding it in place as I zipped up my suit. I walked slowly to the edge of the hangar and stared out over the canopy once more. Thank you Jason, I said to myself. From my feet to the forest and out across the skyline lie a million paths, each of them mine to choose. I won't let us down. I won't let them ruin us.

Ruinus
by Mikell Czermendy

ISBN: 978-0-615-74363-9

Cover image courtesy of lovethesepics.com